BAD HOOKUP

BILLIONAIRE'S CLUB BOOK 4

ELISE FABER

BAD HOOKUP
BY ELISE FABER
Newsletter sign-up

BAD HOOKUP
Copyright © 2019 Elise Faber
Print ISBN-13: 978-1-946140-21-0
Ebook ISBN-13: 978-1-946140-20-3
Cover Art by Jena Brignola

BILLIONAIRE'S CLUB

Bad Night Stand

Bad Breakup

Bad Husband

Bad Hookup

Bad Divorce

Bad Fiancé

Bad Boyfriend

Bad Blind Date

Bad Wedding

Bad Engagement

BILLIONAIRE'S CLUB CAST OF CHARACTERS

Heroes and Heroines:

Abigail Roberts (Bad Night Stand) — founding member of the Sextant, hates wine, loves crocheting

Jordan O'Keith (Bad Night Stand) — Heather's brother, former owner of RoboTech

Cecilia (CeCe) Thiele (Bad Breakup) — former nanny to Hunter, talented artist

Colin McGregor (Bad Breakup) — Scottish duke, owner of McGregor Enterprises

Heather O'Keith (Bad Husband) — CEO of RoboTech, Jordan's sister

Clay Steele (Bad Husband) — Heather's business rival, CEO of Steele Technologies

Kay (Bad Date) — romance writer, hates to be stood up

Garret Williams (Bad Date) — former rugby player

Rachel Morris (Bad Hookup) — Heather's assistant, superpowers include being ultra-organized

Sebastian (Bas) Scott (Bad Hookup) — Devon Scott's brother, Clay's assistant

Rebecca (Bec) Darden (Bad Divorce) — kickass lawyer, New York roots

Luke Pearson (Bad Divorce) — Southern gentleman, CEO Pearson Energies

Seraphina Delgado (Bad Fiancé) — romantic to the core, looks like a bombshell, but even prettier on the inside

Tate Connor (Bad Fiancé) — tech genius, scared to be burned by love

Lorelai (Bad Text) — drunk texts don't make her happy

Logan Smith (Bad Text) — former military, sometimes drunk texts are for the best

Kelsey Scott (Bad Boyfriend) — Bas and Devon's sister, engineer at RoboTech, brilliant

Tanner Pearson (Bad Boyfriend) — Bas and Devon's childhood friend, photographer

Trix Donovan (Bad Blind Date) — Heather's sister, Jordan's half-sister, nurse who worked in war zones, poverty-stricken areas, and abroad for almost a decade

Jet Hansen (Bad Blind Date) — a doctor Trix worked with

Molly Miller (Bad Wedding) — owner of Molly's, a kickass bakery in San Francisco

Jackson Davis (Bad Wedding) — Molly's ex-fiancé

Kate McLeod (Bad Engagement) — Kelsey's college friend, advertiser extraordinaire, loves purple and Hermione Granger

Jaime Huntingon (Bad Engagement) — vet, does excellent man-bun

Heidi Greene (Bad Bridesmaid) — science, organization, and *Twilight* nerd

Brad Huntington (Bad Bridesmaid) — travel junkie, dreamy hazel eyes, hidden sweet side

Ben Bradford (Bad Swipe) — quiet, brooding, had a thing for golden retrievers
Stef McKay (Bad Swipe) — lab assistant, dog lover, klutzy to the extreme
Tammy Huntington (Bad Girlfriend) — allergic to relationships
Fletcher King (Bad Girlfriend) — has a thing for smart, sassy women

Additional Characters:

George O'Keith — Jordan's dad
Hunter O'Keith — Jordan's nephew
Bridget McGregor — Colin's mom
Lena McGregor — Colin's sister
Bobby Donovan — Heather's half and Trix's full brother
Frances and Sugar Delgado — Sera's parents
Devon Scott — Kels and Bas's brother
Becca Scott — Kels and Bas's sister in law
Heidi Greene — Kels' friend since college
Cora Hutchins — Kels' friend since childhood
Fred — the bestest golden retriever in the world*Sir Fuzzy McFeatherston aka The Fuzz* — Jaime and Kate's pet rooster

Kelly S. I couldn't continue doing this without readers like you!
Thank you for having my back and supporting my work. <3

ONE

Rachel

RACHEL WATCHED her boss dance with her second husband—or maybe husband twice over was a better description?—and gave a little sigh of happiness.

Yes, Heather was technically her boss, but she was also her friend.

And her friend deserved a happily ever after.

The party was just getting started, friends and business associates spilling out onto Heather's back patio that had been decorated with twinkly lights, an abundance of flowers, and plenty of portable heaters.

Only the Sextant—herself, Abby, Bec, Seraphina, CeCe, and Heather—along with Jordan and Colin, Abby and CeCe's husbands, respectively, and of course, Clay, knew that the surprise wedding they'd celebrated that night was technically a *second* wedding.

The rest of the guests just thought Heather had pulled a fast one on Clay.

Rachel smiled as she remembered the way the couple had

come down the stairs, both of their eyes a little damp, but love emanating from every fiber of their bodies.

The vows had been beautiful and—

Ugh. She was getting a little too sappy.

Wiping the tears away before they could escape—and heaven forbid, ruin her mascara as Abby was always so worried about—Rachel blew out a breath and set about making sure the food the caterers had delivered was arranged properly.

Soon the cocktail hour would be over, and then the group of fifty-plus—okay, so she knew it was exactly fifty-*seven* guests, because she was damned good at her job—would descend like locusts on the food tables.

Everything needed to be ready.

So, she went down her mental checklist. Appetizers. Check. Several types of salad. Blegh, but check. Entrees. Pasta, chicken, and vegetarian. Check. Check. Check. The cake was also ready, perched at the end of the table and waiting to be cut.

"This little shindig your doing?"

Rachel froze, all her nerve endings going on alert.

She knew that voice.

She knew if she turned around, she would see *him*.

Him.

Tall, much taller than her, but lean when compared to her curves. Still, all that lankiness hadn't meant a lack of strength. He'd been all sorts of hard and hot as he'd pinned her against the door and pounded into her.

Rachel cleared her throat but didn't rotate to face him. "Not my doing. I just helped out."

A long pause, probably because normal people usually looked each other in the eyes when they conversed.

"Well, from what I've seen, you've done *a lot* of helping out." He put a hand on the table next to her, and she shifted away, shivering. She remembered what those fingers could do, how they'd traced over her skin, slipped between her legs, slid *inside*.

Shuddering, she smoothed out a wrinkle on the tablecloth.

"For a last-minute surprise wedding, everything is beautiful," he said, no doubt waiting for her to say something semi-coherent.

She didn't.

Instead, Rachel shrugged and began fussing with the placement of the warming dishes.

The man didn't take the hint. He didn't leave.

Why won't he leave?

She dropped her chin to her chest.

"So," he finally said after another lengthy—and silent—moment. "Gay, taken, or not interested?"

"Oh my God," she moaned, one hand coming up to push her bangs off her forehead. "This is *not* happening."

"I—" A beat then his voice was incredulous. "I *know* that moan." Warm fingers grasped her wrist, tugged until she could see him in all his yumminess.

Her moment of weakness. Her hookup because she'd been feeling desperate and lonely and—

"It's you," he said softly.

Yes, it was *her*. Rachel, the good girl who didn't sleep around, who *certainly* didn't hook up with random strangers in a bar.

Rachel, who *had* hooked up with a stranger.

The sex had been damned good. Incredible, actually.

But it had been just that. Sex. And she hadn't been able to let go of the guilt. She'd now slept with a grand total of two men in her life, and one of them was her husband.

"I—" She tugged at her wrist. "I need to go."

Heather and Clay chose that exact moment to saunter over.

Why universe? Why?

"Rachel," Heather said, closing the distance between them and hugging her tight. "I told you not to work so hard on the wedding. This"—she swept her hand around the deck—"is all too much."

"You deserve to have a beautiful wedding," Rachel murmured to her boss and gave her a quick squeeze before she stepped back.

Heather shook her head, but she was smiling. "Thank you."

"Yes, thank you," Clay said. "For all of it. I know it was a lot of work, but we appreciate—*Oh, good*"—he wrapped an arm around her shoulders, turning her to face Sebastian fully—"I was going to introduce you two, but I guess you've already met my assistant, Sebastian."

Sebastian's expression flickered with shock—no doubt mirroring her own—but luckily, Clay and Heather were too lost in each other and the moment to recognize just how big of a bomb Clay had just dropped.

After a few more words, their bosses moved on to talk with a business associate, and Sebastian's blue-gray eyes darkened. His stare, all heat and desire and sex appeal, was what had undone her the first time they'd met.

But it was his words, the hint of a growl edging into his voice that made her insides tremble in *that* moment.

"I'm *really* looking forward to working with you, Rachel."

She tipped over a bowl of salad dressing.

TWO

Sebastian

HER NAME WAS RACHEL. Somehow the name fit her perfectly.

She was absolutely gorgeous, but in an understated way, with olive skin and deep chocolate brown locks. That hair had tumbled over his hands in long silken waves as he'd sent them both skyrocketing to completion. Pouty pink lips had matched him kiss for kiss, slender fingers had gripped his shoulders tightly as he'd slid home.

She'd been cute in the bar but unbelievably beautiful in the throes of an orgasm.

Sebastian hadn't been able to get her out of his mind since that night.

But she hadn't come back to the bar—or at least, she hadn't returned when he'd been there. And he'd been back to Bobby's *a lot*. There was also the complication of not knowing her name. He couldn't stalk her on Instagram or Facebook, couldn't even look for her on Tinder.

And now she was here, elbows deep in ranch dressing.

"Shit," she muttered, scooping up the mess with practiced efficiency, shifting a plate this way, a bowl that way until the stain had disappeared. Her heels clicked on the composite deck boards as she rounded the table and bent to peak under the floor-length tablecloth.

Fuck him senseless.

Her ass—

Rachel glared at him as she straightened, a fresh bowl and a bottle of salad dressing in her hands. "You're a pig," she snapped.

He raised a brow as she stormed past him. "You don't wear a dress like that"—his gaze trailed down the tight red number, plumping up her breasts until they threatened to spill from the deep V, clinging to her narrow waist, her hips and ass on full display—"and—"

"And what?" She filled the bowl, stomping over to return the bottle back underneath the table, though without the mouthwatering bend this time. "I'm asking to be ogled?"

Sebastian, rather intelligently, he thought, opted not to answer that particular minefield of a question. "You're beautiful," he replied instead. "And freakishly efficient."

Her shoulders, which had been hunched somewhere in the vicinity of her ears, relaxed. "I don't know about the first, but I'm definitely trying for the second."

"You're succeeding."

She pressed her lips together, drawing his gaze to her brightly painted mouth—crimson today instead of pink. Fitting, given her dress, but not helping his concentration. He wanted to kiss it off her.

"So," he said when she went back to ignoring him. "Are we going to talk about it?"

Her hands clenched into fists. "No."

He leaned a hip against the table, rattling the carefully

arranged bowls, but before he could move, she was in front of him, yanking him back a pace.

"So help me God, if you mess this up for Heather and Clay—"

And that was enough.

Sebastian wrapped his fingers around Rachel's arm and began leading her to a private corner of the deck. He'd scoped it out earlier, knowing that this type of socialization was important for his future in the business world, but also just as easily understanding that small talk was taxing for a guy like him.

A guy who had to work for it. Who was naturally awkward and unfunny.

A guy who'd prefer to be the quiet observer rather than the center of attention.

But he wanted to be successful, dammit, and that meant he needed to learn how to play the game. Sebastian just considered himself lucky that Clay thought him smart and talented enough to be willing to teach him the rules of the game.

He would be learning from the master.

Well, the *two* masters, since his boss was lucky enough to be married to one Heather O'Keith. It could be said she was an even more successful businessman than his own boss . . . and that was really saying something.

Rachel's heels skidded on the deck, and he cursed under his breath before slowing his pace.

He'd been warring with himself, thinking only of getting her out of sight in order to kiss that lipstick from her mouth and demanding, coaxing, pleading, okay, *begging* for another night.

He knew he'd fucked up.

But just one more night.

He'd make it good for both of them.

Shit.

Because Sebastian knew he couldn't bring up any of those

appeals. Heather and Clay were the keys to his future. He needed to learn from them, not piss Heather off by screwing with her assistant. Clay was loyal, but he was also pragmatic.

If Sebastian made Rachel angry and then that got back to Heather? Well, Sebastian had no doubt he'd be packing up his corner office at Steele Technologies.

Wife trumped assistant any day of the week.

"Sorry," he said and loosened his grip, gently tugging her around the side of the house so they were out of sight of any of the wedding guests.

The noise of the party muted and shadows danced around them.

This was a bad idea.

Rachel's chest rose and fell rapidly. Her breasts. *Fuck.* He wanted her to breathe just a little deeper, prayed for one of her dusky nipples to pop free. His mouth actually watered for it.

She stepped back, crossed her arms over said breasts. "Not going to happen," she snapped. "They're taped in."

His lips curved. "Well, that's a damn shame."

"What do you want . . ." Her chin lifted, but he knew she scrambled for his name. "What do you want?" she asked, more firmly that time.

"Sebastian," he said. "My name is Sebastian."

A huff. "I *knew* that."

"Did you?"

Olive skin dusted with the slightest hint of pink. "Yes. So why did you drag me over here?"

He hesitated, warring with himself. "Why did you go home with me that night?"

Her eyes flashed to his. "I—"

"I still remember the feel of you coming against my tongue, sweetheart. I can *still* feel—"

Her fingers came up to his mouth, pressed firmly to stop his words.

"We have to work together," she said. "This can't—"

"I know," he said and let himself rub one strand of her hair between his fingers. It was silk, just like he remembered. "*I know*. But that night was . . ."

Her chin dropped to her chest, tugging the lock from his grip. "I can't do this."

"Why?" he asked, suddenly brightening as the obvious occurred to him. They could work together. Their bosses were married, for Christ's sake. "Heather and Clay are—"

Brown eyes flashed up to meet his, regret in their depths. "I'm married."

THREE

Rachel

"I'M MARRIED."

Okay, that was pretty much a technicality at this point, but Sebastian didn't need to know that.

Except, he somehow knew she wasn't telling him the truth.

Or the whole truth anyway.

"There's something you're not telling me," he said, moving closer. Near enough that she could smell the spicy scent of his aftershave, the slightly bitter tang of pine from his hair gel.

She'd nuzzled against that throat, ran her hands through his hair over and over, taking the scent home with her on her fingertips. The smell had teased her for hours and yet she hadn't been able to wash her hands.

Hadn't been able to wash away his scent.

Or maybe she was the one who had actually stepped closer —damned pheromones or hormones or—

"What is it you're not telling me?" His voice had softened, but she wasn't fooled by the quiet tone. There was something ruthless about the statement, almost warning her to not explain herself, to disobey him and see what might happen.

The thought of what *might* happen made her shiver.

"*Rachel.*"

"Nothing." Unfortunately, she squeaked her reply. Literally *squeaked* it out.

And such was her voice on Sebastian.

Her response made his brows yank down, made his stormy blue-gray eyes darken, as if a squall were raging just beneath his surface. And based on the step he took in her direction, the way he reached for her, it wasn't a tropical depression.

It was a category-four hurricane heading straight in her direction.

Shit and *Oh boy* flashed through her mind in equal measures.

"Rach—" Heather's voice cut off as she no doubt took in the cozy little scene in front of her.

Or rather, Rachel seconds from launching herself into Sebastian's arms and forgetting the shame she'd felt after the night they'd shared, the imprudence of having a relationship with someone she worked with, the fact that almost every man on the planet was a giant egotistical asshole.

But, thankfully, Heather's interruption managed to jump-start Rachel's brain.

"Go away," she said, thinking quickly and waving a hand to shoo Heather back in a fashion that was more friend than boss . . . but that was how they rolled these days. Still, Rachel forced herself to keep her tone light, not wanting to alarm either friend or boss. Not when she was barely saving the situation as it was. "Sebastian and I are trying to figure out how to squeeze two more days for your honeymoon from the Berlin trip."

Heather's expression transformed from perplexed and slightly concerned to satisfied. "I knew you two were going to be the ultimate tag team for our quest to take over the world." She rubbed her hands together, evil genius style.

"Oh Lord," Rachel said. "You're too much. Now go. Enjoy the party and leave the plotting to us."

Heather smirked. "Don't work too hard."

"Pot meet kettle," Rachel replied with a roll of her eyes.

"Just remember that playtime is part of the fun."

Rachel felt her cheeks heat. The last time she'd hung out with their group of friends, the Sextant had made it perfectly clear that they thought Rachel was in serious risk . . . of regrowing her hymen. "I remember."

Sebastian raised a brow but didn't say anything as Heather left with a chuckle.

"Playtime?" he asked after they were alone. "Or maybe the more important question is if you're really married then why in the fuck did you sleep with me?"

Now wasn't *that* the question of the hour?

"It doesn't matter," she snapped.

"Like hell, it doesn't." Sebastian was close enough that she could smell the whiskey he'd been drinking on his breath. "You—"

"Fuck. Off," she gritted out. "My life. My vagina. My fucking business. And it doesn't matter because it is never happening again. Got it?"

Okay, so maybe she shouldn't have poked him in the chest.

But, Rachel didn't do too well with men ordering her around.

Not anymore.

He gripped her biceps, holding her still as he glared at her. "It matters because I don't sleep with married women."

"Congratulations," she said, dislodging his hands. "I'll send you a goddamned medal."

He caught her wrist.

"Let me go."

"We're not done here."

Four words that made her temper explode. Admittedly, it had already been fraying at the edges, but she'd heard that particular phrase too often over the last seven years.

Too often to ignore it. Again.

Too often to acquiesce. Again.

Too often to cower. Again.

"Let. Me. Go." She twisted, yanking her wrist from his grasp and executing a breakaway she'd practiced repeatedly.

And then she was free.

Her anger faded almost as quickly as it had come on, transmuting to shocked awareness.

It had worked.

It had actually worked.

Sebastian lifted his hand—

Rachel might have been training in taekwondo and jujitsu for the last eighteen months, might have been working her ass off, learning how to be strong and safe and—

Eighteen months didn't change twenty-six years.

A man lifted his hand and . . . she cringed back.

Silence. Taut and edgy and uncomfortable.

Sebastian dropped his hand and bent to meet her eyes, and she had to force herself not to recoil away from him, from that blue-gray stare that saw too much. "I wasn't—" he began. "The tape— I was just going to fix your dress."

She swallowed, eyes stinging now. "Yeah."

More silence.

Her arms were aching now, and Rachel was mortified to realize they were curled next to her head, protecting her brain, her face. She'd been taught that . . . just not from her karate instructor.

She'd been trained to cover her face from her father, from her husband.

Otherwise she ended up with bruises that were difficult to explain away.

But no more. It was why she'd finally summoned the courage to leave. It was why she worked for Heather O'Keith, the biggest, baddest female CEO around. If Rachel just took one percent of what Heather did and said to heart, then she might one day find herself normal and complete.

Not the half alive being that had slipped from her Iowa home in the middle of the night with just the clothes on her back and hadn't looked back.

"I don't hit women."

She forced her arms down to her sides. "I wasn't worried you would."

Lie.

"I—" He shook his head. "Fix your dress."

She glanced down at the bodice of her dress, saw that fashion tape or not, she was dangerously close to a wardrobe malfunction. Sebastian averted his eyes as she tugged everything in place.

"Thanks," Rachel said once all her body parts were safely stowed.

Her embarrassment was growing with every passing moment. She wanted to go home, wanted to get away from Sebastian, from the careful way he now looked at her.

She'd ruined all her progress with a single cringe.

How humiliating.

"I'll squeeze those two extra days out for the bosses' honeymoon," he said. "You can go."

Saw. Too. Much.

She lifted her chin. "I'm fine."

"No," he said, shaking his head. "No, you're not."

Rachel opened her mouth to argue. Pointlessly, since obviously, he was right. She *was* seriously fucked up. "I—"

He sighed. "See you at the office."

And then he was gone, taking her pride, dignity, and confidence with him.

Another lie. Because she'd lost that particular trifecta many years before.

FOUR

Sebastian

SEBASTIAN PROPPED himself on the fringes of a circle of chatting wedding guests. Close enough that he could appear to be involved in the conversation, but distant enough that no one was going to try to draw him in or force him to actually contribute to the dialogue.

He didn't know anyone aside from Clay and Heather, and even his boss's wife could hardly be considered more than an acquaintance at this point.

Normally, he would have made himself put on the charm, practice some of the skills he was learning and honing due to Clay's help, but today he just wanted to be invisible for a little while longer.

Plus, he couldn't focus on holding his own when Rachel—

There.

She emerged from the corner of the house, dress straight, expression placid.

Her stride in those sexy-as-fuck heels was steady and her smile when she reached her group of friends was wide.

Of course, it was also fake as hell.

Which he definitely shouldn't know, but he'd seen her real smile, experienced it firsthand that night in the bar a few months before. And he remembered it because the simple quirk of her lips had elicited a very *not* simple response in him.

Heart pounding. Hands clenching. A yearning deep inside—

And fuck him, now he sounded like a romance novel.

But he had this hole inside of him, an aching emptiness that never seemed to be filled, no matter how hard he worked or how many contracts he snagged or how many hours he spent at the office.

He was empty.

Except that night, he'd almost felt full.

A woman with bright red hair wove her arm through Rachel's and tugged her more firmly into their circle. Sebastian knew the woman was Cecelia Thiele—or formerly Thiele, anyway, as she had married Colin McGregor, Heather's business partner.

He watched and waited as her friends laughed and talked a mile a minute, but he didn't relax until Rachel joined in, finally gracing the group with a real smile.

Then he breathed.

Finally.

He slipped free of his group before heading toward the back door, ready to escape. No one was paying him any attention and it was easy to bypass the pockets of conversation, to slip inside. His neck prickled as he moved further in, becoming surrounded by the dim light of the kitchen.

He glanced back.

Lights twinkled over the deck, little pockets of bright that competed with the setting sun as it shone through the windows.

Sebastian was fully in the shadows, but the awareness didn't leave him.

Not when he could see Rachel through those plates of glass, observe her watching the house with unmasked concern. There was no way she could see him inside since the windows were all tinted with UV reflective coating. Clay had arranged, or rather Clay had paid and Sebastian had coordinated the installation on Heather's windows when one of their new business investments had recently perfected the process. The coating was said to reduce energy loss by almost ninety percent.

In other words, Clay had invested in another soon to be billion-dollar corporation.

The man was a fucking genius.

Rachel watched the house for nearly a minute until one of her friends said something that drew her attention back to their group.

Her gaze flicked toward the house only once more and he didn't have to be a fucking genius to see that she was beyond relieved he hadn't stepped back out.

Shaking his head, he headed down the hall and out the front door.

He'd go back to the office. At least he could make heads or tails of things there.

Fuck. She'd actually thought he was going to hit her. The look in her eyes as she'd cowered—pleading mixed with the purest form of fear he'd ever witnessed. And then her expression when she'd realized what she'd done. Disgust, humiliation.

As beautiful as she was, he hadn't been able to look at her, not when she so obviously hadn't wanted to reveal that side of her.

Not when she was so vulnerable and hating every goddamned second of it.

He'd looked away.

And now he wished he hadn't. Why couldn't he have told

her it wasn't her fault? That *no matter what,* no one should have—

He unlocked his car and slid inside. She didn't want him to wax poetic on what was right or wrong. She certainly didn't want him nosing further into something that was obviously so painful.

Nothing he said would change what had happened to her.

"Fuck!" he yelled and punched the steering wheel hard enough to make his hand ache. "Fucking hell," he said, softer, after spending a minute staring out the window and trying to make sense out of the whole fucked up scenario.

She was married.

The bastard hurt her.

Sebastian had slept with a married woman.

For the first time in years, he'd felt whole. Because Rachel was gorgeous and amazing and sweet and shy and so fucking responsive. She'd been out of place in the bar—sophisticated, kind, and funny in a sea of normal. He'd considered himself so fucking lucky when she'd invited him back to her hotel room.

But then Clay had called with an emergency and he'd had to go into the office to sort it out.

It had been a doozy, a mix-up with an intern sending the wrong documents to a prospective investor and nearly torpedoing all hope of a deal. Sebastian had fired the intern then had personally flown to L.A. with the proper documents in order to rescue it.

He'd been on the plane, heading home at nearly one in the morning before he realized that he'd forgotten to leave a note.

Or find out Rachel's name.

But he'd gone back to Bobby's every chance he got, hoping to run into her again, hoping to make it up to her all while assuming she'd been in town for a business trip or quick vacation—hello, hotel room—and had gone back home.

Little did he know that this was Rachel's home.

So why the hotel room?

And why hadn't he gotten her name?

It had been a funny little joke between them, a shared smile when some pathetic excuse for a man had tried to pick her up. She'd dismissed him and he'd taken a chance by chiming in from the other side.

"Don't worry, my name doesn't rhyme with cock, I promise." She'd turned and he'd nearly swallowed his tongue. Model beautiful, but skeptical eyes.

They had softened upon meeting his. "Luckily for me, mine doesn't either."

Then they'd spent the next hour talking about bad pickup lines in bars, favorite movies—*Pride and Prejudice* for her, *Die Hard* for him—books, and Netflix.

When she'd invited him back to her place, fuck if he'd been prepared to decline. The most beautiful woman he'd ever met, who'd kept him laughing with snarky comments about bar scenes and cheesy Netflix documentaries—Who knew that Flat Earthers were a thing?—had wanted him to leave with her.

Sebastian would have had to be stupid not to accept.

He was a lot of things, but stupid wasn't one of them.

Rachel was incredible and . . . someone had hurt her.

He started his little Toyota, carefully navigating through the minefield of a driveway filled with Mercedes and Land Rovers and Bugattis, and pulled out onto the highway.

His rage barely contained, he forced himself to keep the pace safe, forced himself to drive carefully to the office. If there was one thing he was good at, it was control. He'd control himself for the time being, channel this fucking anger into something productive.

But he damn well was going to find out who hurt Rachel.

And then he was going to kill the son of a bitch.

FIVE

Rachel

"HE'S GONE," CeCe whispered.

Rachel straightened, tried to play it cool. "Who's gone?"

One red brow raised. "The yummy slice of man meat who disappeared with you around the corner not too long ago."

"Nothing happened." Her cheeks felt hot even though it was the truth. Nothing *had* happened, that day anyway. And she also wasn't counting her . . .

Well, she could say with all sincerity that cowering before him was much more humiliating than sleeping with the man. He might have fucked and run, but that was what she got for picking him up in a bar, no matter that she'd thought Sebastian different.

So yeah, she was going to excise the memory of her cringing before a man when she'd promised herself that she would never, *ever* do that again, and she was just going to pretend it hadn't happened.

Rachel was really good at that.

"We know nothing happened," Seraphina said, all blond

and buxom and gorgeous. She was also incredibly kind and had taken Rachel under her wing in recent months, extending dinner dates and movie nights when the other girls were busy with their husbands or in Bec's—another one of their friends—case, being too swamped with work to hang out.

"Yup," Bec chimed in. "Lips not swollen. Hair in perfect, shiny, bouncing"—a glare from the high-powered attorney—"curls. Bitch, you'd better share your fucking secret. My frizz is real."

"Humidity is not your friend, especially in Iowa during the summer. I had to learn fast." Rachel forced herself to keep her tone light even though the mere mention of her home state caused her heart to pound.

She'd promised no more hiding.

Not now that the divorce was almost finalized.

"Ugh," Bec said. "You're so"—she swept a hand up and down—"beautiful."

Sera snorted.

"And you," Bec added, "have no room to talk. It's like the two of you were vomited up from a shampoo commercial. Oh look, I'm so gorgeous and bouncy and—"

"That's twice she's mentioned bouncy," CeCe said, lips twitching.

"Oh, Bec." Sera patted her arm, affecting an overly sympathetic tone. "You're emotional from the wedding, aren't you? Poor thing. So many feelings."

Bec glared. "Shut it, you."

"That's more like it," CeCe said.

"What's more like it?" Abby, their ringleader and Heather's sister-in-law, swept into the circle with her son, Carter, on her hip. "What'd I miss?"

Sera grinned. "Bec has *feelings*."

Rachel's lips twitched and Abby couldn't hold back her hoot

of laughter. Bec narrowed her eyes at them, but then Carter reached for her and she backed up in panic.

"Oh, no." She raised her hands up. "This is Armani. It doesn't do babies."

Rachel rescued her by snagging Carter as he almost leapt from Abby's arms in an effort to get to Bec. She smiled down at him then made a silly face. "Aunty Bec is just a big ol' scared baby, huh?" She glanced up. "They're like cats, you know? They sense weakness and pounce."

Abby's hazel eyes danced with amusement. "Did you just call my son an animal?"

She pointed down at the onesie Carter was wearing. It was emblazoned with the words, "Party Animal."

"Case in point." Her eyes flicked back to Bec, who, speaking of pouncing, looked ready to circle around and jump back on the fact that Rachel had emerged from a shadowed corner of the deck only minutes after Sebastian.

Or maybe that was just her imagination.

Regardless, Rachel wasn't about to let the conversation come back to her.

Down that path led madness.

Or perhaps retribution, she thought after she'd raised Carter's arm and pointed it in Bec's direction, saying, "Let's go back to why Bec has feelings."

Considering the death stare her friend shot her, Rachel had a *feeling* that payback would very much be in her future.

THE EMAIL CAME LATE that night.

Mission accomplished.
-S

Rachel sat on the couch of her new apartment, a lovely little space just a few blocks from RoboTech's San Francisco offices. It was above a bookstore, which if she were truly being honest, would have been enough to sell her on the place, lovely original wood floors and slightly larger than a postage stamp kitchen aside.

She even had managed to squeeze in a washer and dryer, which after living in her previous crappy apartment for almost a year, was a luxury she reveled in.

No longer would she need to haul her unmentionables down the street to the laundromat. Hell, she could wash her bras in the comfort of her pajamas with Netflix streaming in the background.

Which she'd been about to do, albeit with a much-earned glass of wine, when her inbox had pinged with a message.

Rachel had opened it immediately.

Heather might have gotten better about the sheer volume of her work hours, thanks to the addition of Clay, but she'd been a demanding boss for too long for Rachel to ever risk shutting off her phone.

Though, she should have realized that even Heather wouldn't be emailing Rachel on her wedding night.

Smiling at the thought of Clay banning Heather from her phone instead of pondering how to respond to Sebastian, and it *was* Sebastian, she reasoned, seeing that the address it came from was sebastianscott@steeletechnologies.com, Rachel opened and closed the foldable stand on the back of her cell.

It popped in and out. In and out.

She wondered what Clay's expression would be when he saw the lingerie the Sextant had picked out to kick off their married life, round two. It had even made Bec blush, and Bec was about as hard ass as they came.

Hard. Ass.

Snort.

Oh dear Lord, she was getting to be as bad as the rest of them.

And . . . none of this was helping her email reply.

She could just say, "Thanks" and leave it at that. But simple gratitude was also a little boring, and she didn't want Sebastian to think she was boring.

So, what to say?

"Awesome, see you soon!"

Blegh. That was way too chipper.

"Well done."

Not his boss, so could be read as condescending.

"Nailed it."

What, was she a nine-year-old?

In the end, she didn't have to come up with anything. Her inbox pinged with another message that made her heart skip a beat when she read it.

I can smell the smoke from here. Don't worry. I've included the details below so you can review and approve. I hope this Saturday night finds you safe and with a serial killer documentary streaming in the background.

-S

P.S. Yes, this is Sebastian

P.P.S. I won't bring up what happened . . . any of it.

P.P.S.S. But I still wish you'd never experienced whatever it was that put that much hurt in your eyes. Your smile lights up the room.

Rachel blinked back tears.

Fuck. Why did he have to be nice?

And this addendum to his previous message brought her no

closer to the light, witty response she'd been attempting to come up with.

Ugh. Why was she overthinking this?

Uh, because he'd seen her at her absolute weakest and she didn't know how to make his impression of her go back to how it was before. If she could only come up with something funny or clever enough, maybe he'd forget that she'd been cowering like a pathetic—

No.

She wasn't weak or pathetic. Not anymore. She'd left Iowa and come to California to make a new life in a place that she'd always dreamed of living.

That took big ol' lady balls.

Rachel was the current owner of giant lady balls. *See.* That meant something. She could come up with a humorous little email. No problem. Of course, she could—

Her inbox chimed again.

No response needed. Good night, and enjoy your doc.
-S

Okay, seriously?

The man did not play fair.

I haven't started it yet. The Killer Chronicles, join me if you dare.
-R
P.S. This is definitely Rachel, mainly because my name is in the email.

Ha.

Beat that Sebastian Scott.

Unfortunately, or maybe fortunately for her, he did.

SIX

Sebastian

SEBASTIAN GLANCED AT HIS PHONE, read Rachel's response, and smiled.

Considering what he'd found out during the last few hours, he shouldn't be smiling, shouldn't be feeling amusement, but Rachel had struck again and he somehow found himself grinning at the pert email she'd sent.

Rachel Morris was technically still married.

But what she had neglected to tell him, in what was both an extremely quick-thinking and wholly effective way to keep him at a distance, was that she was not so much married as nearly divorced.

As in the divorce paperwork had all gone through, both parties had had their say—or at least their lawyers had—and the date of finalization was less than a month out.

So, married.

But just barely.

Which begged the question of why she'd told him at all and had him circling back to the notion that she'd done it to push him away. Sleeping with a married woman would tend to make the average guy back off.

Except Sebastian didn't consider himself average.

Ego, much? he imagined his sister Kelsey saying.

Okay, yes. But he'd worked hard to become the person he was, had put in hours transforming himself from the quiet nerd who'd been too afraid to chime into a conversation into a confident businessman.

So a little ego was warranted, at least as far as he was concerned, *and* Rachel being married for just twenty-six more days didn't particularly concern him.

Not when he considered how she'd reacted to him lifting his arm, not when she'd thought he was going to strike her. He'd seen dogs cower the same way, knew it took many instances for their reactions to be so honed and instinctual.

Someone had hit Rachel, and it had been more than once.

Also, it didn't take a genius to figure out that her former husband, Preston Johnston, was the likely culprit. He'd had a multitude of police reports filed against him for assault, but no formal charges brought by the local Iowan DA from the town that Rachel had grown up in.

Hardly any effort had been required to hack into the police department and the district attorney's records and even less to track down the records mentioning Rachel. From there, his source had discovered Rachel's husband's name.

Despite Mr. Preston Johnston acting the part of a good church-going man and reveling in his roles as a pillar of the community, Sebastian had dug up plenty on Rachel's ex.

Sixteen reports of assault and battery from a variety of sources—former employees, restaurant staff, even several former girlfriends—but the instances that had made his blood really boil were the five reports filed by Rachel.

They'd come with pictures.

Of Rachel bloodied and bruised, with busted lips and black-ened eyes that had been so lacking in emotion, she could have been a corpse.

And considering some of the injuries, especially those from the final report, Sebastian was half surprised she *wasn't* dead.

Preston had beaten the shit out of her. He'd also never paid the price for it.

Sadly, it had taken Sebastian longer to find the two extra honeymoon days they'd promised their bosses in the Berlin trip's itinerary than for his source to access the records that were supposed to be private. It had only taken one call to the former Steele Technologies employee, who now specialized in doing exactly the kind of research that was just shy of being illegal, but which many business owners relied on to make sure their invest-ments and prospective employees had been vetted properly.

It was beyond inappropriate that he'd used those services on Rachel, but Sebastian couldn't find that he gave a shit.

He'd needed to know the truth of why she'd reacted as she had and . . . he was going to find some way to make Preston Johnston pay.

No one should ever be allowed to do what he did and get away with it.

His phone buzzed with an incoming email.

Too scared, Bas? Afraid this little documentary about a guy who killed and then ate his victim's corpses will give you nightmares?

Well, put it that way.
He rolled his eyes and typed back.

I am man, hear me roar. I'm not scared of no kill-or.

Oh fuck, that was bad. But the thought of his horrible attempt at a rhyme making Rachel laugh or even just smile a little bit, had him pressing the send button.

Yes, it was horrendous.

No, he didn't care, so long as it made her burden a little lighter.

Also, that—wanting revenge upon her ex, wanting to make Rachel happy—was going to be a huge problem. He knew it, he could foresee it disrupting all his carefully laid out plans, but he couldn't stop himself from skipping down that particular path with a bucket of daisies held in his hands.

And *that* particular metaphor was going to stay firmly locked in his skull.

Her reply came only a few seconds later, in the form of a GIF with a hysterically laughing baby tipping backward under the force of its laughter.

His own lips tipped—up, not backward.

He also couldn't resist trying his hand at adding another line to his poem, which he gave a perfectly horrible name.

> *Men who Roar . . . or Maybe Purr*
> *I am man, hear me roar. I'm not scared of no kill-or.*
> *I am man, hear me purr. I'm only scared of a dude using my skin like fur.*

And . . . send. Sebastian imagined her bursting into laughter, the sparkling sound that had made his night so much better in the bar. He anxiously awaited her email in response. Something pert about him being terrible? Another GIF?

But he waited long minutes and nothing came through.

Score zero for his rhyming abilities—

Ping.

I am woman, hear me roar. I need to eat ice cream-a-four?
Clearly, I'm even less talented than you at rhyming. I'm pressing play on my murderer doc in thirty seconds.

Sebastian sank onto the couch and cued up the movie. He had a shit ton of work he should be doing—emails that didn't involve horrible poems to return—research to complete for his proposal to Clay, logistics to solve with his boss being out of the office for an extended amount of time.

But instead, Sebastian put his feet up and hit play just as his internal counter passed thirty seconds then he pulled out his phone and sent:

You'll have to explain all the big words to me.

Rachel's reply didn't disappoint.

I am woman, I'm not scary. I can be your dictionary.

SEVEN

Rachel

MONDAY MORNING FOUND her back at the office.

Saturday night, well also the wee hours of Sunday morning, should have been a distant memory.

That poem.

Lord. They'd added so many horrible lines to that poem.

And yet, as they'd finished the first documentary and moved onto a second and then a third, Rachel couldn't remember the last time she'd had so much fun with a man.

Not ever, if she were being truthful.

Her father had been a terrifying creature, only bringing pain and fear for the three months out of the year he'd been home. Something that she'd considered a blessing then as well as now. She'd at least been able to escape him *some*times.

Of course, without a mother and having a father who'd been gone three quarters of the year, meant she'd stayed with family.

With her grandparents.

Her father had hit her, had pushed her around more than a

few times, but it was her grandparents who'd seriously damaged her psyche.

They'd been there day in, day out.

And they'd been determined that they stamp out any lick of her "whore of a mother."

The church and religion had been their weapon.

They'd wielded it masterfully.

Rachel blinked, realized that she'd been sitting in her office, staring at her computer screen for at least ten minutes. She was losing it. Seriously. But between the divorce and Sebastian and all the feelings he invoked, she was losing her freaking mind.

It was the timing of it all. Everything was still so fresh and confusing. On one hand, she was relieved to be almost free of Iowa and Preston and her family and the memories. On the other side, she had friends at home that she missed.

The church community had been both a blessing and a curse.

Just because her husband and grandparents had used religion as a way to control and punish her, didn't mean that the rest of her church had been bad. She'd had so many of the members bring her meals when she'd been "sick" as Preston had declared to the congregation. They'd given her so much of their generosity—cleaning her house, doing her laundry, filling her fridge with food.

But they hadn't helped her get out.

For the longest time, she'd held that against them.

Now, she understood they didn't know how much of a snake Preston was.

She'd been fooled during their courtship, and of course, they had been fooled as well. They didn't live with him. They didn't experience the unpredictable violence of his mood swings. They didn't—

A knock at her office door. "Rachel?"

Luckily, she'd gone back to staring at her computer screen, rather than out the window, when the interruption made her jump. At least she'd given the appearance of doing *something*.

"Yes?" she said, swiveling her chair so she faced the intruder.

Her arch tone made Brian, their newest intern, pale. "I-uh —" He swallowed hard, and she took pity on him.

"Come in and sit down." She gestured to the chair in front of her desk. "What's going on?"

He walked in slowly and sat. "I'm—uh—"

Okay, she understood he was new and that he was probably nervous and wanting to do a good job, but the kid seriously needed to finish that sentence.

Her brow lifted when no further words came. "Today, please."

"I wanted to know if I could take Friday off?"

Rachel pressed her lips together in an effort to stop her sigh from escaping. She'd been two seconds from diving straight into crisis mode, and Brian wanted to take a day off?

"You have PTO days," she said. "Use them. Just make sure to finish the rest of your work before you take off."

He nodded and relief made his shoulders relax. "Thanks. I know I'm new here, but the snowpack is looking really good this time of year and I want to—"

She raised a hand. "Too much information." He shut up. "Now please make sure the Pearson, the GloGlobal, and the Cruz reports are finished and on my desk by ten."

"But it's eight thirty now," he said.

Rachel pointed to the door. "So, I guess you'd better get moving."

Brian's head went full on bobblehead as he all but ran for the door. On the threshold, he hesitated then said, "Oh. I forgot to mention, someone from Steele Technologies is here to see you. I think he said his name is . . . Sebastian?"

Shit.

She was woman, hear her run. She couldn't bear to see that particular some*one*.

Double shit.

She couldn't face Sebastian. Not today.

Flicking her eyes back to her computer screen, she waved a dismissive hand. "Tell him I'm busy."

"I—uh—"

There those words went again. Brian really needed to remember how to use them.

But the next voice stole her words right alongside Brian's.

"Not going to get rid of me that easily, Morris."

Her gaze shot up, and she saw Sebastian leaning against her open door, arms crossed casually, one foot resting over the other. A smirk teased his lips.

"Speechless?" he asked. "Didn't think that was possible with you."

Brian shifted, clearly wanting to escape.

"Move, Bas," she said. "Brian has work to do."

"Invite me in, why don't you?" Sebastian walked past Brian and sank into the chair in front of her desk.

"Shut the door," she told Brian as he all but sprinted from her office. It clicked closed a second later.

"Bas?" Sebastian asked, all sexy male and though he was confined to the chair, it somehow didn't do anything to lessen his presence in her space. His scent trickled through the air, teasing her senses with hints of pine and spice. She'd thought him rangy before, teetering toward lean, but occupying the same area that Brian had just vacated indicated how wrong she'd been about his size.

He wasn't bulky, but he also wasn't small in the least. He

filled out his suit remarkably well, and the phrase that kept popping back into her mind was that he had a quiet strength.

There wasn't any tumult radiating beneath the surface, no mean streak lurking, *waiting* for the right opportunity to lash out at her.

Or . . . he hid it really well.

"Sebastian is too long," she said, glaring when his lips twitched. "Don't take it too deep."

His brows rose, a snort escaped. "Long? Deep?"

She groaned and leaned back in her chair. "You're not serious, are you?"

"It made you smile."

Rachel felt her cheeks creasing into said smile and realized he was right. "You're a juvenile." A beat. "And why would you want to make me smile, anyway?"

He went very still in the chair, and quiet stretched between them as he studied her. Finally, he relaxed back and crossed his arms over his chest. "You're beautiful when you smile."

She froze. "I . . ."

"And, for the record, I like when you call me Bas." He pulled out his phone, holding it in her direction and adding quickly, "I know you're busy, but I'm here to exchange numbers and coordinate calendars."

Rachel forced herself to focus—on the calendars, not the fact that she'd had to play off the fact that she'd given Sebastian a nickname without even realizing it . . . and that she hadn't even played it off very well.

"How do you want to manage them?" she asked instead of commenting on the fact that he liked her calling him Bas. "Keep their separate calendars for each of them but add one joint calendar that we'll both have access to?"

"Works for me." He made a note in his phone. "Do you handle all of Heather's scheduling?"

She nodded. "For now. She wants to move me over eventually to help coordinate some specific projects so I don't get stuck in the administrative assistant track."

Not that Rachel would have minded.

She enjoyed organizing things, tucking them all away into their proper cubbies, fitting in meetings, streamlining her boss's day so Heather could accomplish more in a shorter amount of time. Work smarter, not harder, and all that.

Though Heather could hardly be accused of not working hard.

"What about you?" she asked Bas—*Sebastian*. "Do you want to remain Clay's assistant?"

Because she was curious and wanted to learn more about him, okay?

It was stupid, but she wanted to know what made him tick. Things like—did he often meet up with chicks in the bar and go back to their places? Or maybe, why had he disappeared without a goodbye?

That last one had hurt most of all. But it did make more sense after discovering that he worked for Clay Steele.

She, herself, had dropped many a plan when something desperate had come up with Heather.

But that night had been—

Well, it had been the first time she'd really put herself out there since her marriage.

She'd taken a risk and been burned.

Rachel had been celibate for so long and even before that, sex had been a control tactic for her soon-to-be ex, for her grandparents. They'd controlled what she'd read, watched, even what she'd worn, and the slightest hint of cleavage or a shortened hemline had invoked all types of lectures about her fall into whore-dom.

There had been no personal expression.

And then Preston.

God. He'd seemed like her savior at first. So charming, so sweet. Oh, there had been many red flags, but she'd been desperate to get away from her father, from her grandparents.

She'd jumped from the pan into the fire.

He'd controlled it all and even with sex he'd decided when and where, how long, whether or not he'd bring her pleasure or . . . well, if there would be pain instead.

But that had been the past and she'd been determined to move on. So, when Bec and Sera had invited her to meet up with them for a drink at Bobby's, owned by Heather's brother, who was aptly named, Bobby, she'd gone when normally she wouldn't have.

Bobby's had two rooms—a back bar area for the "older" crowd and a front space filled with the youngsters. Her gorgeous friends had been inundated the moment they'd stepped into that first room. Of course they had, Sera was stunningly beautiful and too kind to reject even the creepiest soul, but Bec had stayed by Sera's side, de facto wingman, and had waved Rachel into the back room.

Which was where the really cool kids hung out.

Or at least where she and her posse of grown women who laughed at inappropriate jokes like twelve-year-olds and teased each other relentlessly tended to congregate.

He'd been there that night, sitting on a stool pulled close to the worn wooden bar, a glass with amber liquid in his hand.

And for some reason—*okay*, because he'd drawn her in even then—she hadn't gone into the Sextant's usual booth.

She sat at the bar.

"God no," he said and she snapped out of her memories and scrambled to remember what they'd been talking about.

He'd asked and then she had—

Oh. She'd asked if he enjoyed being Clay's assistant.

"I like Clay, a lot," he said. "And I don't mind the role for now. He's taught me so much. But"—he sighed—"I want to be doing more, you know? Find something that I can really sink my teeth into."

It was the sigh that did her in. He just looked so earnest yet unsure that her heart went full squish.

He was sweet. He was one of the good ones.

She stood and crossed to the front of her desk, leaning back against it. A lock of his blond hair had fallen across his forehead and her fingers itched to push it back into line.

Instead, she said, "You want something that isn't flight schedules and hotel points?"

He watched her, blue-gray eyes as soft as her heart felt. There was something about this man, about them together that just made sense. Like they were old souls or reincarnated, or lovers in a former, okay, in *this* life.

But draw or not, attraction or not, one glorious night of multiple orgasms or not, she was married—

Excuse.

Fine. Almost not married.

It didn't make a difference. She was damaged goods. Rachel had a past that made her, if not suspicious of the opposite sex, then at least not open to a relationship with one.

Yes, there were good men out there—Jordan, Clay, Colin, and despite his disappearing act, even Sebastian—but she . . .

She what?

Didn't deserve one?

That was bullshit.

Everyone deserved to feel safe and loved and cared for.

But . . .

Her throat tightened.

No one had ever really loved her. What if there was something, not wrong exactly, but what if she was broken or missing something that normal people had?

Or what if she was just unlovable?

Fingers on her cheek made her jump.

"I'm going to kill him."

Her eyes flashed open.

Sebastian was on his feet, expression furious.

She almost did it, almost scuttled backward in fear.

But then she remembered his poem and somehow, somehow, her mouth curved up into a smile. "I am man, hear me roar. The only thing I fear is your dirty, dirty underwear." She bent over, ridiculous, inappropriate laughter bursting out of her.

Bas wouldn't hit her.

She didn't know *how* she knew, just that deep down in her heart of hearts, she understood that he was one of the good ones.

But then she remembered what he'd said.

She straightened. "You're going to kill who?"

Guilt swept across his face.

Wobbly legs took her around her desk, managed to line her ass up with her chair before they gave way. The cushion of cool leather did nothing to calm her temper.

"Sebastian Scott, you did *not* background check me."

EIGHT

Sebastian

OKAY, so he'd fucked up.

Sebastian winced. "It's not like you think—" he began.

"So, you *didn't* background check me?" Rachel stood again, hands plunking onto her desk as she leaned toward him.

Pink colored her cheeks and those brown eyes had darkened to espresso.

Fury absolutely radiated through every line of her body.

It was a beautiful thing to witness.

If only *he* hadn't been the one on the receiving end of that death glare.

"Well . . ." He hesitated.

"That's not a no," she gritted out and straightened, crossing her arms over her chest. The motion plumped her breasts and drew his gaze. Literally, he couldn't *not* look there. "When did you—" She snapped her fingers. "Eyes up here, Sebastian."

He blinked but dutifully raised his gaze. "I'm sorry," he said, already sad about the fact that she stopped calling him Bas.

"For what?" she asked, lips pressed together. "For the background check or the inappropriate looking?"

"There isn't really a good way for me to answer that question." He rose to his feet, crossing around the desk to stand next to her. "You're beautiful, and I think I made it clear that I wouldn't turn down another night with you."

Rachel's chin lifted. "I thought I made it clear that I would."

"Ouch." Sebastian risked touching her shoulder, a gentle brush of his fingers that was as much of an apology as his words. "I shouldn't have done the background check. I knew it was wrong, but I still did it anyway."

She retreated a step. "So why?"

"Because you said you'd been married and then behind the house . . ." He clenched his hands into fists, wanting to reach for her, to tug her close and hold her tight, to make her ex a distant memory.

And he didn't have that right.

So, he told the truth instead. "I was worried that you were still in danger."

There. He'd said it, and if she were still mad at him about the invasion of privacy, then he'd accept her rage as well earned.

But Rachel didn't get mad.

Nope. She burst into tears.

She bent in half and sobs wracked her body. And finally, Sebastian didn't think any longer, didn't resist. Instead, he crouched down and pulled her close. He sank to the floor and rested back against her desk, holding her tight as she cried.

"Aw, baby," he murmured. "Don't cry. I'm sorry I did that. It was wrong of me. But you also don't have anything to be ashamed of. Your ex is a disgusting excuse for a human being who deserves to have his entrails torn from his body and—"

She sniffed and shook her head. Her sobs changed to slightly hysterical laughter. "I'm sorry," she cried. "I just—I had the inappropriate thought that you've been watching too much *Game of Thrones*."

His lips twitched and he leaned back enough to meet her eyes, to wipe the tears trailing down her cheeks. "I really am sorry."

Rachel bent and wiped her face on his shirt.

He grimaced but figured it was penance for his overstep.

"Oh damn," she muttered, straightening again and wincing at the wet spot on his button-down. "Sorry. I didn't think. I'll pay for your dry cleaning. I—"

"It's fine," he told her. Snot aside, he kind of liked that she wasn't thinking about her interactions with him, that she was just reacting. "I didn't like this shirt anyway."

She snorted.

"Are you—" Sebastian hesitated to bring up the background again but figured it was best for both of them to clear the air completely. "Are you okay with . . .?"

She sighed. "I wasn't—I'm *not* crying because of the check. Or, I guess I am. I mean . . . I am pissed about that. But"—she tilted her head up toward the ceiling—"I guess I'm crying because no one has ever cared that I was in danger before."

His brows pulled together.

"It wasn't just my ex who was abusive. It was my dad, my grandparents." When she glanced back down at him, her smile was fragile. "You don't even know how big of a treasure trove of fucked up you've stumbled upon."

"Rach—" he began when she pushed up from his lap.

"No." She raised a hand when he reached for her. "Might as well make it clear, yeah? My mom left. My dad was a real asshole, but lucky for me only home for a few months out of the year. My paternal grandparents raised me and while they didn't hit me like dear old Dad did, they managed to fuck my head up so much that I married Preston, thinking he was my safe way out." A brittle laugh. "And Preston was worse than all of them combined, but I guess you already know that since you've seen the police reports."

"Why—?" He clamped his mouth closed, knowing the question he'd been about to ask wasn't fair in the least.

She guessed it anyway.

"Why didn't I leave?" Rachel sighed and turned away from him, walking over to the windows that looked out onto San Francisco. "I've asked myself that a million times," she said softly. "And I *did* leave at first. But I didn't have a plan, and my grandparents wouldn't take me in. I had a few friends, but I was scared to . . . it would be a lie if I said I didn't go to them only because I was scared that Preston might hurt them. That was a concern, of course, but I didn't go to them because I was ashamed."

Sebastian carefully moved to her side. He didn't touch her, not when she was holding herself so tightly that it seemed as if a feather could shatter her. "What could you possibly have to be ashamed about?" he asked as gently as he could.

Rage was flooding him, pulsing through every cell and nerve. He needed to punch something, to put his fist through a wall, to break something for no reason except to unleash this fury that was ripping him apart from the inside out.

But Rachel needed him calm, needed to excise this darkness that was bogging her down.

"Because I went back." Her hands rose, and she adjusted the low ponytail gathering her hair at her nape. "Because I was weak. Because I didn't report every time. Because I only did report him when I was forced to by the police." She dropped her chin to her chest. "Not that it mattered. Preston's father was an attorney in the DA's office. Not easy to get charges to stick there, and things were always worse after one of those reports."

Sebastian swallowed hard, trying to control himself, trying

to make his expression placid so that when she looked at him, she didn't fear him.

She couldn't *ever* fear him.

"When nothing changed after that first report, I knew it was only a matter of time before he killed me. He was too strong, too violent. It was—" Silence then a long, slow breath. "I knew I had to get out and I had to go far. But Preston controlled everything —credit cards, cash, bank accounts—so it took a long time for me to save up enough money to leave. Still, eventually I did and so I picked the place that was pretty much the farthest from home and ran."

Rachel rotated to face him, and her eyes were empty for a long moment. They were like those pictures, dead and disturbing and cold—

But then they warmed and she reached her hand up, cupping one side of his face.

"Thank you for being furious for me, Bas."

And fuck, did that break his heart.

But it also leashed it . . . only to her.

NINE

Rachel

WHOOMP, there it was.

She'd laid it all on the table, so let the man judge her or run far, far away.

That was the typical reaction when someone revealed the amount of emotional baggage she carried around, right?

But instead of running screaming out of the room, instead of calling her weak or stupid—when she struggled not to call herself those things—he placed his palm over hers, keeping her hand on his cheek.

"Confession."

Her heart stopped.

Oh God, *why* did her heart stop? It had no business stopping like this, for a man, for a man's *touch*.

Not for a woman like her, with her past.

One half of his mouth curved up. "I like it when you call me Bas."

She blinked. "What?"

"I've never had a nickname before." He shrugged, and the slightest bit of a flush might have colored the tops of her cheeks. "That was more of my brother's specialty. Being cool enough to have a fun nickname that is."

"Did you just counter my story of abuse with a lament about you missing out on a cool childhood nickname?"

He paled. "Shit. I didn't mean it that—"

Rachel bit back a grin. "I was joking."

Sebastian—*Bas* glared. "That is *not* funny."

"So, I shouldn't joke about the bad shit that's happened in my life?"

Obviously, everything that had happened to her still hurt and, frankly, she often woke in a heart-pounding panic in the middle of the night, half-expecting to be back in that house of horror in Iowa, Preston bent over her, fists raised.

But she'd learned a lot from being lucky enough to make friends that she knew would stand by her, no matter what. Hell, she'd gone hat in hand to Bec months before, knowing that she couldn't afford the other woman's legal fees, but needing help when Preston had contested their divorce.

Bec hadn't blinked an eye and she'd refused to accept anything more than a new pair of the cozy but ridiculously expensive pajamas they all adored wearing in payment for her services.

Rachel would have bought her a hundred pairs if her friend would have accepted them, but Bec hadn't helped her for pajamas or money or even thanks.

She'd helped Rachel because they were friends.

Rachel had never been part of a group like the one she'd stumbled into after beginning to work for Heather. They'd accepted—okay, more like yanked—her into their fold and Abby, CeCe, Sera, Heather, and Bec had been nothing short of amazing. Loving, judgment-free, supportive, and . . .

They'd taught her how to laugh.

How to laugh at herself, her situation, her love life, or lack thereof.

And while she hadn't burdened them all with the exact details of what had gone down during her childhood and her marriage to Preston—Bec aside, who'd needed to know everything for the divorce—they all knew that she'd left something pretty shitty back in Iowa and had been looking for a fresh start in California.

"I think you should do whatever you want to do," Sebastian said, hand flexing over hers. He drew it over to his mouth and pressed a soft kiss on the center of her palm, then laced their fingers together at his side. "It's your life, Rachel. All I want for you is to live it and be happy."

She'd learned humor from her friends. They'd also shown her that sometimes life provided opportunities to leap, to live . . . to love. Her friends had grasped those chances, sometimes diving fearlessly, other times tentatively tiptoeing in.

But they'd lived and found happiness.

And in that moment, Rachel thought that she could, too.

There was just one other thing, something she'd already assumed to understand, but also she needed to know for sure.

With all the mistakes she'd made with Preston, she needed the confirmation that her instincts about Sebastian were right. So she sent a mental plea to the universe, hoping that those assumptions were right and then asked, "Why did you leave that night?"

His cheeks went pink, and he grimaced. "An intern fucked up a deal." He raised his hands, palms out, hurrying to add, "Not an excuse, at all. I know I should have woken you or at the very least I should have left a note." Regret was laced into his words. "You don't know how often over the last few months I've been kicking myself for not getting your number. Or hell, your name."

"Why didn't you?"

"Clay likes things to move and move fast. I got word that things were going south with the deal and panicked. I booked it into the office and then on a plane to L.A." He winced. "It wasn't until I got everything sorted out and was heading home in the middle of the night that I remembered . . . I did go back to the hotel the next night, but you were gone. Unless you have something to tell me and you're really into hairy dudes who answer the door in their briefs?"

Her heart squeezed even as her mind revolted against the image.

"I'm really sorry," he said. "I should have led with that. I just . . . everything else."

She nodded. "I get it, Bas."

His relieved breath was loud. "I promise it won't—"

She rose up on tiptoe and slanted her mouth across Sebastian's.

He froze, pulled back. "No, sweetheart. You don't have to do this."

Moving so that her front was more fully against his, she said. "I thought you wanted me to live my life and be happy."

"Yes, but . . . that doesn't have to involve—"

"You?" she asked, brow raised. "But what if I want it to involve you? What if you're the first person in my life who has cared what I want? What if I say that I lied before and that I'd like you to be my friend?"

Stormy blue eyes collided with hers. "Friends don't kiss." A brow lifted. "Unless Clay has something to worry about with all those girls' nights your crew of troublemakers has been organizing over the last months."

She smirked. "You wish."

A shrug. "Maybe. You are all gorgeous, but that's not my point. You've been through a lot and you shouldn't rush—"

"I'm going to interrupt you and I'm *kind of* sorry for it," she said.

"Only kind of?"

"Yes. Because again, it's my life. If you don't want me or feel pressured or uncomfortable pursuing a friendship because of Clay and Heather, I get it." She shrugged, playing at casual but knowing that if he didn't want to spend more time with her outside of work, it would hurt. For the second time in her life, she was truly trusting her gut.

The first had told her to leave.

This time it was telling her to leap.

His hands came up, weaving into her hair, sliding the strands of her ponytail through his fingers. "I'm not feeling pressured," he said and tilted his hips so that his pelvis was flush against hers.

And *oh,* how she remembered the feel of that particular body part.

"I think that tells you just how *not* pressured I'm feeling at the moment," he murmured. "But I also know you've been hurt and I don't want you to jump into something that will put you at risk."

Rachel pressed a kiss to his jaw. "And what about you? Aren't you worried I might hurt you? That I'm just using you to rebound from my marriage?"

He rolled his eyes. "I'm a big boy. I can handle myself."

Men.

She tapped his cheek. "Now repeat those words except substitute girl for boy."

His expression went chagrined. "I see your point."

"So, can we get back to kissing now?" She glanced down at

her watch. "I have fifteen minutes before I need to go back and terrorize my intern."

He grinned. "I like seeing you as the boss."

She laughed. "That's Heather, but I do my part."

Fingers trailed down her nape, sliding around the slip under the collar of her shirt, to tease the delicate skin at the base of her throat. Bas chuckled, the warm puff of air on her jaw so close yet so far from where she wanted it.

"So, what you're telling me is that I need to do my part?"

Her teeth found her bottom lip, and she bit down when he nibbled at her earlobe. "You're going the wrong way," she breathed. "I'm over here."

"I see you," he said and she had the feeling that, yes, he actually did see her.

Then his mouth was on hers, and she could think of nothing but the way he kissed—like a fucking god, for the record—how his tongue felt stroking against hers—hot and wet and dizzying—and how incredible it was when his body pressed tightly to hers.

It was like that night again. One touch and she lost her mind. The only thing that made it bearable in any way was the fact that Bas seemed as crazed as she was. He groaned and pulled her somehow closer, hands running down her back to cup her ass.

And *fuck* did that feel good.

He hitched her up, and she wrapped her arms around his neck, her legs around his hips, moaning as he pressed her back to the window.

Heaven help her if anyone looked up from the street below, but *fuck* could she summon enough concern to ask him to stop. Not when his cock was hard and pressed against her, rocking in a rhythm that made her see stars.

The only thing that would have made it better was for them to both be naked and Bas inside her, but since that would require more than fifteen minutes and more privacy than her office allowed, Rachel would have to settle for this.

Not that she was complaining. *This* was damned good.

At least until her phone rang.

Bas tore his mouth from hers.

She grabbed his face, tugged him back. "Just one more minute," she begged.

"One minute," he agreed and kissed her again.

Approximately zero point two seconds later his cell began buzzing. And while she didn't mind the vibration, considering that the pocket housing it was in a very prime location, she knew their moment had ended.

Her cell cut off then immediately began ringing again. Bas's was still buzzing.

"Honeymoon's over," she said.

His lips twitched as he lowered her legs to the ground. The way he held on to her for a second, ensuring that she was steady and didn't instantly fish out his cell warmed her heart.

"Apparently," he said, wry amusement in his tone before growing serious again. "You okay?"

His phone stopped buzzing. Then straightaway began vibrating again.

"I'm great," she said and for once, felt like she'd actually answered that particular question honestly. She swept across her room and picked up her phone. "You ready for this?"

Bas slid his gaze down and back up and though the man didn't touch her, Rachel would swear to God that she could actually feel that stare. Her skin heated and suddenly her mind wasn't on her boss or the phone in her hand but back on launching herself into his arms.

"Don't look at me like that," he growled.

She released a shaky breath. "Don't *you* look at *me* like that."

His mouth quirked and the heat faded from his expression. "Only if I get a rain check for later."

She slid a finger across her phone screen to accept Heather's call.

"As if that were ever in question."

TEN

Sebastian

THE PHONE CALLS from Clay and Heather turned out to be less crisis and more work-related. Apparently, their bosses weren't great at taking time off and those two extra days he'd managed to squeeze out of their work-slash-honeymoon trip to Berlin had gone to waste.

Well not entirely to waste, since Clay had accidentally hit the FaceTime button causing Sebastian to see—

He shuddered.

A view he definitely couldn't *un*see.

He'd quickly promised to get the ball rolling on researching a new start-up while Rachel dealt with a case of encrypted files that had somehow become corrupted.

His call hadn't taken long and he watched Rachel unabashedly as she held her cell pinned between her ear and her shoulder all while talking a mile a minute and typing furiously on her keyboard.

She was magnificent.

Her eyes flicked up and pink colored her cheeks as her gaze quickly returned to her computer screen.

He spied a pad of Post-Its on her desk and a pen and took a moment to jot out a quick note that he propped in front of her.

Do you want me to go?

Chocolate eyes dashing up to meet his then a nod that had his gut clenching.

Damn. But he'd asked and so he obeyed. He stood, started to turn away only to halt at her hand movements.

She gestured for the pad and pen then wrote furiously when he passed them over.

I don't want you to go. But you're distracting, and I really want to finish this so we can meet up later.

He was distracting?

Sebastian felt his chest puff up. He'd take that, along with the whole meeting up later thing.

Another Post-It appeared in front of his face.

Only if you want to.

He grabbed another pen, snagged the paper back. He wrote:

To meet up later or go?

A smile.

Either. Both.

"Oh—" She jumped, glanced down at her desk. "Okay,

Heather," she said. "I'll ping your inbox once IT takes a look at those files. Uh . . . yup. Bye."

Rachel hung up and set her phone carefully beside the stack of Post-Its. "I —uh . . . I think that I just heard Clay . . . *um* . . ." This time her cheeks didn't go pink so much as fire engine red.

"Were they having sex?"

She shook her head. "No. But they definitely are going to be having it in short order."

He snorted.

She snorted.

And then they were both laughing.

Fuck, did that feel good.

Eventually they got themselves under control, and he found himself crossing around her desk again and crouching in front of her chair.

"I'm not going to kiss you again," he said, smiling. "Since we both know where we'll end up." He stroked the outside of her thighs, forcing himself to keep his hands on the outside and not in between. *Fuck it.* He allowed himself just one touch. And it was so worth it.

Rachel's breath hitched, and a moan caught in her throat.

"Did Heather sound like that?"

A nod.

"*Fuck.* I want to put my mouth on you so bad, baby." Then he groaned when she spread her legs just the tiniest bit wider.

Her lips parted.

"Don't," he said and kissed her. Just once, but enough to make it count, to hold him over until later. Only when his lungs screamed for oxygen did he pull back and cup her cheek.

She nuzzled into his palm and Sebastian's heart softened even further. This woman. God. He just liked her so much.

"Give me your number," he said.

Her eyes smiled. Which didn't really make sense, but

somehow they brightened and pure happiness radiated out of those chocolate depths.

She punched her number into his phone, pressed send. "There."

He kissed her nose, because he could and because he didn't trust himself to take her mouth again. Not when his mind was already flooded with images of him stripping off those tight little slacks, unbuttoning her blouse and undoing that tidy ponytail then bending her over her desk.

He'd drop to his knees, make love to her with his mouth until she screamed his name. Then he'd slide in deep and—

"I'll see you later?" she asked.

Sebastian clenched his hands into fists for what felt like the umpteenth time that hour, but the action did the trick. He didn't reach for Rachel and strip her naked.

Instead, he managed a semi-controlled sounding, "I'll see you later" and showed his horny ass out her office door.

But he couldn't resist sending her a new line once he'd reached his own office.

I am man, hear me cater. I can't wait to see you later.

Her response was a pert GIF and the reason he wore a smile for the rest of the day.

ELEVEN

Rachel

LUNCH BREAK MEANT that she called in the help of the Sextant . . . or at least the member who was the closest and knew the most about Rachel's particularly screwed up situation.

"Darden," Bec answered curtly.

Rachel didn't take the greeting personally. Bec was a powerful attorney whose work ethic rivaled even Heather's. She also didn't take calls from, in her words, "People she gave less than two shits for."

So if she picked up a call, and this was doubly true for an answered phone during normal work hours—which for Bec was basically six o'clock in the morning until eight at night—then it meant she'd allowed the caller entrance into her inner circle.

Jackpot.

"Molly's? I'll bring it to your office," Rachel asked.

"I would adore Molly's," Bec said.

Molly's was a sandwich and salad restaurant and pretty much the only place in the city that made vegetables and so-called health food palatable, at least according to her and the rest of the Sextants. Yes, vegetables were a necessary addition in a balanced diet, but they were also an evil one. The little cafe was one of Rachel's spots, somewhere she'd stumbled upon in the early days after arriving in San Francisco.

She'd felt lost and overwhelmed and painfully anonymous. But it had also been the best feeling in the world.

Because she'd been free.

And she could order clam chowder just because she enjoyed it and not worry later about Preston detesting the fishy smell.

She could order *anything*.

"So when are you coming by, my little born-again virgin?"

"Forty minutes work?" Rachel asked before pausing then figured why the hell not. "Also, about that born-again virgin thing . . ."

"Holy shit," Bec said. "You'd better make it thirty. I'll just take that salad thing."

Rachel rolled her eyes. "Which salad thing? The pear and brie or the apple and cranberry."

"Either. Both. I don't care," Bec said. Rachel grinned, loving how her friend's New England accent took over when she got excited. The words were clipped and rapid, and she sounded half *Real Housewives*, half New York socialite. "I need to hear more about your vagina."

Okay, maybe more than half *Real Housewives*.

"It's—" Rachel broke off. "Well, Bec, it's pretty fucking complicated."

"A sigh and a curse word," Bec said and Rachel could swear she heard her friend rubbing her hands together in gleeful anticipation. "This is going to be good."

"Probably." Rachel pushed open the door to Molly's.

So, she'd already banked on Bec saying yes to lunch.

The food was really that good.

"I'm hanging up now," she said.

"Thirty minutes," Bec replied. "And you're going to spill all your secrets."

"As if I could withstand the Darden Death Stare," she joked.

"Damn right." Bec disconnected the call, and Rachel found herself smiling as she headed up to the counter to order.

Good friends. A potential beginning of something with a new guy. Maybe friendship, maybe more—friends with benefits, boyfriend?

Who knew?

But there were possibilities and those were something Rachel had lived without for a long, long time.

She would take her chances grasping at every single one of them.

"So, was he good?"

Rachel thought that her smile said it all. Especially, when Bec hooted and dropped her fork.

"Holy shit!" She clapped her hands together. "Little Sebastian really has *that* much going for him?"

Rachel smirked. "He's got enough, but better yet, he knows how to use it."

"Hot damn." Bec picked her fork back up and shoveled a bite of salad into her mouth. "I never would have guessed. So, what's the problem?"

Rachel thought about that for a long moment. "Nothing really." She shrugged. "Which I guess is kind of the problem. I thought I'd freak out the first time after . . . you know . . ."

"And you didn't?" The Darden Death Stare didn't come out, but just having Bec's gray eyes fixed on her made Rachel spill her guts.

"No," she said. "I didn't freak. I wanted more. But he'd disappeared." She scooped up a bite of her own salad. "Later I got it. I mean, I've up and left things at the drop of the hat just because Heather called. But even when I hated him for leaving, I still wanted him. *God*. Does that even make sense?"

Bec nodded, serious for once. "Yeah. I get that feeling completely."

Rachel froze with her fork two inches from her mouth. "Why do I feel like there's a story there?"

A wry smile. "Because there is, but it's not one I'm going to tell you. Or anyone, for that matter." She waved a hand dismissively. "The only pertinent thing is that I was young and stupid and naïve."

"Been there, got the freaking T-shirt," Rachel muttered.

"We're part of the same club, apparently." Bec rolled her eyes. "But no freak out. That's a good thing, Rach."

She picked at her salad, searching for another crouton. "I know."

"Then what's the real issue bouncing around that brain of yours?"

"I just—" Rachel sighed. "Ugh. I *like* him, okay?"

Bec snorted. "Woman. That's a *good* thing."

"But what if—"

"Ah." Bec nodded and pushed away her food, fixing her eyes firmly on Rachel's. "I get it now. You're scared Sebastian might be more than a quick fuck."

Rachel made a face. "He's already more than that."

"Well then, I think you already know how to resolve your problem."

"I do?"

Bec grabbed her plate back. "Sure. You see where things go with Sebastian. You keep an open mind. You prepare for either alternative."

"Either?" Rachel parroted.

"Look, Sebastian is a good guy. He doesn't have any police reports, convictions, or lawsuits." Bec ticked off the words on her fingers. "He's never even gotten a speeding ticket. His brother is a retired NHL player, his sister a brilliant engineer. His parents are still married and live in a middle-class suburb."

Rachel's mouth dropped open. "How do you know all that?"

Bec shrugged. "I had him checked out when I found out he was Clay's assistant."

Oh. Em. Gee.

Rachel bit back a giggle.

Bec had background-checked Sebastian.

That was somehow too perfect.

"What?" Bec asked, mouth full and the word sounding like "Shmut?" She chewed and swallowed before saying, "He was going to be near Heather, and no one messes with my O'Keiths."

"I love you, Bec."

"Damn right you do." She paused. "So, you either accept that Sebastian will be around for a good long while or you cut him loose now."

Rachel thought about that carefully. "I don't think I can cut him loose."

A flash of a smile. "Well then, I guess you had better get used to Sebastian being around then, don't you think?"

The thought of Sebastian being around on a potentially permanent basis made Rachel's heart feel buoyant for the first time in forever.

She grinned at Bec.

"I guess I'd better."

TWELVE

Sebastian

HE'D BEEN LOOKING FORWARD to later all day and now *later* seemed like it wouldn't be coming.

Sighing, Sebastian pulled out his cell and called Rachel.

She answered after three rings. "Hey, you." Her voice was soft and made what he was about to tell her all the more painful. "How's it going?"

"I'm knee-deep in a crisis."

"*Oh.*" She sighed. "I'm guessing that means we won't be meeting up?"

Sebastian dropped into his desk chair, head pounding, feet aching from running all over the city. "I'm sorry."

"Don't apologize," Rachel said, her voice taking on a stern quality. "Shit happens. I'm disappointed is all." Her tone softened. "I was thinking about you all day."

He liked the sound of that. "Yeah?"

"Yeah." Heels clicked across the floor and he heard a *snick*.

"Did you just close the door?"

A giggle. *God* that sound. He loved making her laugh.

"So, what if I did?"

His phone chimed and he glanced down at the screen. Rachel was FaceTiming him?

He accepted the call.

Her beautiful face appeared on his cell. She was smiling and her eyes held no small amount of mischievousness. "Hi," she said and waved.

His lips twitched. "Hi."

Brows pulling down and together, she said, almost accusing, "You look exhausted."

Sebastian rubbed his temple. "I *am* exhausted, honestly. We had a deal blow up today and the details of the offer shared with competitors." He sighed. "Then the media. Of course, it was skewed to make Steele look bad, like *we* were the ones to torpedo the contract when really the other party was the one to pull the plug."

Her lips pressed flat. "Was this for the tech center for the city?"

Shock pulsed through him. "How do you know about that?"

"RoboTech considered making an offer, but we have our hands full with other charitable projects."

"That's right. The joint venture with McGregor Enterprises. Last I heard, you guys had proceeded to some field testing?"

She nodded. "Now's my turn to ask how you found out about that." Her eyes sparkled with amusement. "I guess our bosses are sharing more than just pillow talk."

"Apparently," he said with a chuckle. Two minutes talking with Rachel, and his head had stopped pounding.

"So, I'm guessing that Steele made a good deal. Why did the city back out?"

"We got tired of the red tape. They wanted us to complete another environmental review—and we've done two already.

Then additional seismic calculations and—" He blew out a breath. "Well, it just got to be too much. So, we said they either went with our initial offers and previous reports or we would walk."

Rachel wrinkled her nose. "So, they went to the media."

"That's the game."

Her heels clicked back across the floor and he saw her computer was still on as she rounded her desk. "I'm not the only one burning the midnight oil," he said. "Why are you still at work?"

She grinned. "I was waiting for someone to call. Or text."

His stomach twisted. "Shit, sweetheart. I'm sorry. I—"

"I'm *joking*." White teeth nibbled the corner of her mouth. "But I do have something that might make you feel better."

One brow rose. "What's that?"

She lifted her hand to her collar, her fingers flicking one button open.

"Uh . . ."

Another button came loose, then another until Sebastian could see the slightest hint of black lace.

"*Fuck*," he groaned. "*That* was what you were wearing earlier?"

A trail of fingers across her chest. Her voice dropped to a conspiratorial whisper and she licked her lips. "This is what I wear *every* day."

He went hard. Just like that, his feet no longer hurt, his head didn't throb. The only thing that was aching was his cock, desperate to be back inside her. "Baby," he groaned. "You're killing me."

"In the best way, I hope." Her hand crept lower, slipping under the lace, pulling it down enough to flash him a hint of one dusky nipple.

"Why are we both still in our offices again?"

She chuckled. "I have no idea," she said and slowly extracted her fingers. He wanted to groan but didn't know whether in disappointment or relief.

Disappointment. Definitely disappointment.

Rachel nodded. "What I *am* going to do is finish up my work here then go pick up takeout. *Then* I'm going to text you my address and the code for my apartment." She glanced down at her watch. "I figure that gives you about two hours to get the crisis under control before heading to my place."

This woman undid him. He liked her so much and wanted to tell her exactly that, but what was between them was so fresh and new that it was too soon for any kind of declaration. And so he floundered, struggling to find something funny to say, something that would illustrate her importance without making her run away screaming.

And it couldn't be another line for their horrible poem.

He frowned.

"Or not," Rachel said. "Bas, if you think—"

"No, that's not it at all," he hurried to say. "It's just . . . you're too good for me, sweetheart."

She snorted. "You do remember my past, right?"

If she'd been in front of him in that moment, he would have been half-tempted to take her by the shoulders and shake some sense into her. Obviously, he *couldn't* do that, either in person or through the phone, but he still wanted to find a way to make her understand that she was perfect and incredible, beautiful and kind—

He wanted her to be his.

But she also needed to become *hers* first.

"Too. Good," he said again. "I'm just the little brother who works as an assistant when my siblings are a professional hockey player—retired now—and an obscenely smart engineer. Like insanely smart. As in Kelsey filed for her first patent at thirteen."

Rachel smiled. "That sounds like . . . a lot?"

He nodded in agreement. "Yeah. I'm the abnormal one because I'm average in smarts and drastically limited in athletic ability."

"I can think of one particularly *not* average thing you've got going for you."

He waggled his brows. "Yeah? Typing a hundred words a minute is an impressive skill, I know."

"I'm wet just thinking about it."

He choked.

"So, see you in two hours?"

Bas nodded mutely.

"Good. If you're on time, I promise you'll get to see the rest of my underwear."

He slumped back in his chair after she'd clicked off, mind spinning all sorts of dangerous and unproductive fantasies of Rachel's underwear.

That woman was going to be the death of him.

Unfortunately, he didn't know at the time how accurate that particular thought would be.

THIRTEEN

Rachel

RACHEL JUGGLED the bag of Italian food—extra garlic bread, for the win—along with a bottle of wine and her briefcase as she keyed in the code to her apartment. It unlocked with a *click,* and she nudged it open with a combination of one knee and her elbow.

Then almost dropped the bottle of wine.

"Super graceful as always," she muttered, closing and locking the door behind her.

Her phone rang just as she was setting the food on the counter.

Thinking it was Bas, she answered without looking at the number.

"Hey, you," she said.

"You've been a bad girl."

The blood in her veins froze solid at the sound of Preston's voice. "I believe there's a restraining order in place that makes it illegal for you to call me." Thank God her voice was steady, that

Bec had warned her this might happen and had coached her on what to say. "I'm hanging up and calling the police."

He snorted. "You wouldn't dare."

"Do yourself a favor and lose my number, Preston. We're done."

"We are *not*—"

Rachel pressed the end button.

Her heart pounded and jumped as her phone immediately began ringing again. *"Fuck."* She jabbed at the ignore button, immediately clicking over to her contacts and pressing Bec's number.

"Twice in one day, my little not-virgin," Bec said. "To what do I owe the pleasure?"

"I—" Her cell clicked in her ear, signaling Preston trying her for the third time.

In a heartbeat, Bec's tone went from teasing to serious. "What's wrong?"

"He—" Rachel sucked in a breath, forced herself to release it slowly. "Preston called me. He's still calling me."

"Did he threaten you?"

"No. I didn't give him a chance. Just told him he wasn't supposed to call me and that I was contacting the police."

"Good. Good." She snapped out an order to someone in the background. "I'm going to call my contact at the PD, then I'm coming over."

"No. I'm okay," Rachel said. "It just shook me, I guess, to hear his voice after so long."

"You shouldn't be alone."

Rachel's gaze went to the bag of takeout on her counter, the bottle of red wine. "Sebastian's coming over."

A pause.

Then, "Good on you, Rach."

"Is this an incredibly stupid idea?"

"Trusting a man?" Bec asked. "Or trusting *this* man?"

Considering the only man she'd trusted before was currently blowing up her phone after having spent close to five years systematically destroying every good part of her.

She had finally got her shit together, finally started to feel like an actual person.

And Preston.

And Sebastian.

"Either. Both."

Bec hesitated again then said, "Trust is a tricky thing, yeah? I've only met the man a handful of times, and my gut says that Sebastian is one of the good ones. But, Rach, the more important question is what does *your* gut say?"

Rachel sighed and studied her toes. "My gut says that, too."

"That's enough for now, don't you think?"

She chuckled. "Is that your patented Darden mic drop?"

"No," Bec said. "It's already hard enough to maintain my copyright on the death stare."

"Oh, Bec," Rachel groaned. "What the hell am I going to do?"

Her friend released a puff of air that rattled through her cell. "You're going to let me handle this. Block the number Preston is phoning from, but don't delete any messages or calls. And definitely don't pick up any numbers you don't recognize." A beat, amusement slipping into Bec's tone. "And enjoy your wild night of hanky-panky with Sebastian."

"I don't even know what that means."

"Oh, you will. You. Will."

Rachel smiled despite herself. "Was that supposed to be the mic drop?"

"I'm just getting started—"

"Well, *I'm* hanging up now."

"Have hot sex—"

Rachel clicked off, somehow smiling despite her past cropping back up, despite Preston's calls still buzzing in her ear.

She really did have the best of friends.

<hr>

SEBASTIAN KNOCKED BEFORE PUSHING open Rachel's door just over thirty minutes later.

He took one second to survey her apartment—a small one-bedroom because real estate prices were insane in San Francisco —then focused his gaze on her.

"What's wrong?"

She pulled out the plates of takeout she'd been warming in the oven and shrugged. "I'm fine."

Bas was by her side in a second, taking the plates and setting them onto the counter. "Bullshit. What happened?"

Rachel sighed. "Preston called. Has *been* calling pretty much nonstop for the last half an hour."

"Did he threaten you?"

She shook her head. "I didn't let it get that far."

"What should we do?" he asked when her phone lit up with another missed call. "Contact the police?"

"Bec's doing that for me."

"Darden?"

She nodded.

"Well, I don't think you could have a better lawyer."

"I agree. And we have a restraining order, so there's not much else I can do at this point."

Sebastian took the bottle of wine when she extended it toward him, along with the opener. "So, serious question now. This"—he gestured between them—"is new and . . . a lot, I guess. Is it too much? Do you want me to go?"

"First of all, that's two questions."

He cupped her cheek and her throat went tight. She sniffed.

"Second, fuck, Bas. You can't say things like that."

"For the record, I like it when you say my name."

Her lips curved. "I know you do." She stepped closer, resting her palm over his heart. "Also, would you—I mean, *could* you stay for a little while?"

He kissed her forehead. "I can stay however long you need me."

Rachel had the feeling that could possibly be forever.

FOURTEEN

Sebastian

HE HELD Rachel as she slept and it was pretty much the best thing ever. It definitely wasn't the end to the night he'd been expecting.

Sex.

He'd been expecting lots and lots of hot, sweaty sex.

Three months' worth of fantasizing, of making up for having to leave her that night . . . and he'd ended up just holding her as she slept.

But fuck if he could find the strength to care. Bas wouldn't have made love to her, even if she'd asked. No way would he force something or risk their future being tainted by her fucking asshole of an ex.

So, they'd eaten takeout and watched two documentaries and stayed up way too late, considering it was a Monday and they still had the rest of the work week to get through.

Around midnight he'd made motions to leave, not wanting to keep her up when she needed rest, but Rachel had said, "Stay."

He didn't have one single iota of strength to deny her anything.

They'd gone into her bedroom and she'd slipped into the bathroom, emerging in a pair of silky pajamas that did nothing to hide her gorgeous body beneath. He'd stripped down to his boxer briefs, borrowed a toothbrush to clean his teeth, and then had slid into bed next to her.

It was domestic. It should have felt awkward considering how short of a time they'd truly known each other.

It hadn't.

Instead, getting ready for bed, cuddling up next to her under the covers, smelling the fruity tones of her shampoo as she'd nuzzled into his neck . . . all of it had felt exactly right.

She'd fallen asleep a few moments later and Sebastian had been left thinking about everything that had happened over the last few days.

His phone buzzed and he glanced over at the screen, saw it was a text from Kelsey.

Carefully, he slipped an arm free and picked up his cell.

Coming to town. Thursday. 6 pm. Dinner with Devon and Mom and Dad.

Great, he thought and planned on scheduling a meeting during just that time. His family meant well, but God were they hard to take in large doses.

Devon would be his usual self, garnering an audience of adoring fans as his wife, Becca, teased him about it. Kelsey would have a brand-new project that would change the world.

And he'd just managed to squeeze out two extra days for Clay and Heather's honeymoon.

Streamers would fly, balloons would drop from the ceiling, so great would be his accolades.

Another buzz.

You're coming. Even if I have to drag you out of your office myself.

He sighed.

I have plans already.

As predicted her response was:

Cancel them. This is important.

Mentally, he weighed his options. Would she actually come to his office and make a scene?

Yes.

Absolutely, she would. And revel in every second of it.

Sighing, he texted back.

See you Thursday.

Her reply came half a second later.

Damn right you will.

With that auspicious ending, Sebastian set down his phone and closed his eyes. But with Rachel next to him, he found that despite the need burning through him, despite Kelsey's decree, and even despite Rachel's past refusing to stay in the fucking past, where it belonged, he was able to close his eyes and fall headlong into sleep.

He woke to sunshine blinding him and Rachel's ass pressing against his cock.

Okay, he had been wrong the previous evening, waking with Rachel cuddled up to him, her warm, sleep lax body in his arms, *that* was the best thing ever.

She rolled over, her hand dropping to his chest then lower.

Well, *that* was definitely the direction he wanted her fingers to travel, though after the events of the previous evening this probably wasn't the best time.

He snagged her hand, bringing it up to his mouth to kiss her palm. "Wake up, sweetheart," he murmured. "Before I forget that I'm trying to be good."

"Mmm." Rachel rocked against him and—*shit*, why was he trying to be good again?

Sebastian closed his eyes. Because it was the right thing to do.

Fuck.

He brushed back her hair, pressed a kiss to her cheek. "Rachel, baby. It's time to get up."

She sighed and, after a long moment, opened her eyes.

"There you are," he said softly.

A smile teased her lips. "You stayed."

He shrugged. "You asked."

"I don't want to get up." Her nose wrinkled.

Bas chuckled. "Me either."

Another sigh. "So how soon until the bosses figure out we're playing hooky?"

"Sooner than we want them to, probably." The strap from her tank top had slipped down her shoulder. He fixed it.

Rachel blinked. "You know, most men would have taken that the other direction."

He slipped from beneath the sheets and stood. "Maybe." A peek under the floral patterned comforter covering her. That was followed by a stifled groan. "No, not maybe. That's a definite."

"So why aren't you in bed with me?"

He grabbed his slacks and stepped into them. "Because it's seven thirty on a Tuesday morning, and we both need to get to work."

One brown brow rose. "No, that's not it."

Bas had begun buttoning his shirt when Rachel slipped out of bed.

Fuck.

He whipped around.

Those fucking pajamas were all but transparent in the morning light.

Fingers down his sides, arms trailing around his middle, breasts pressing firmly against his back. "We should wait until you feel—"

"What?" Rachel slid around to his front and picked up his hand. Then she did something that he never would have predicted and was pretty much the hottest thing ever.

She spread her legs wider and brought his hand into the waistband of her pajamas.

Heat. Wet heat. He couldn't have stopped his fingers from flexing, from sinking into her damp center, from circling the hard bud of her clit.

And he couldn't stop himself from capturing her moan with his mouth.

Soft lips against his, a darting tongue that teased and danced, a lithe female body straining against his hand.

Sebastian stopped thinking and finally, just reacted.

He tossed Rachel onto the bed, pulling her pajama bottoms and underwear off in a single movement.

Then he all but dove for her pussy.

She groaned as he flicked his tongue over her clit then

writhed as he trailed his tongue down one thigh and up the other. "You taste so fucking good," he said and slipped one finger inside.

She bucked. "Fuck, Bas!"

He started to make a snarky comment along the lines of, "Yes, please," but then she shifted and her tank top slipped again, revealing one puckered nipple. His mouth watered to taste it, but since that was otherwise occupied, he reached up, sliding his hand over the silken skin of her abdomen, cupping the soft globe of her breast, and pinched her nipple between his thumb and forefinger.

Rachel screamed and grabbed his head, but instead of pushing him away, as he'd half-expected, she gripped his hair tightly in both fists and thrust her pussy against his mouth.

He took the hint, moving his tongue faster and with more pressure, slipping another finger inside.

She moaned again and Bas thought it was pretty much the best sound on the planet.

He couldn't resist watching her face as she rocked against him—eyes slammed shut, breath coming in gasps, pink dusting her cheeks.

She was beautiful. So damned beautiful.

And then she was . . . almost there, crying his name out on an exhale as if it were a prayer, a benediction, a curse.

He slid one more finger inside and she exploded.

Bas had been wrong again.

That was the best thing ever.

FIFTEEN

Rachel

SHE'D LOST all sensation in her legs.

Literally.

The only thing Rachel *could* feel was her vagina, and that was limited to a warm fuzzy, *good* feeling that also managed to radiate upward to her heart.

Okay, so her Bas-driven orgasm was wreaking havoc on her adjective use, but the man was a fucking god in between the sheets.

Or on top of them, since they hadn't bothered to actually slip between them.

But back to the problem with her heart.

As in Bas's ability to weasel his way past her defenses. She really should be panicking, right? This feeling, this intense longing for him, for this moment to be something that led to adjectives like long-term and permanent, not to mention nouns like future and relationship, *should* be scary.

She'd experienced nearly all the ways permanent, long-term relationships could go wrong.

And yet, this thing with Bas was different.

There weren't any warning signs, there wasn't that sinking feeling in her gut telling her to stop this before it got out of hand.

In fact, her gut was telling her to leap.

That she'd managed to live through the bad and should grab the chance for good, for *Sebastian*, firmly with both hands.

"You okay?" the man himself asked.

Rachel's eyes were still closed, but she reached a lazy hand in the direction of his face. Stubble teased her palm before he pressed a kiss there. "I'm great." She forced herself to peel back her lids. "This is where I would expound on the merits of your skills, but I can't feel my legs."

Bas jumped off her. "Shit, I'm sorry," he said.

"No." She pushed up, grabbed his shoulders, and plunked herself in his lap before he could do something stupid like get out of bed. "That's a good thing, baby. You licked me so good that I forgot I even *had* legs for a minute there."

"Oh." He grinned.

"Yeah." Rachel nipped his throat. "I figure we have maybe twenty more minutes before we risk being *really* behind today or discovered by Boss One and Two, so I think we should make the most of it."

"You don't have—"

She shifted on his lap, the hard jut of his cock both a tease and an ache . . . as in she'd be walking with an ache later today after it had been inside her. Biting back a snort, knowing that the Sextant had thoroughly corrupted her mind, Rachel leaned up and whispered, "I don't *have* to do anything. I want you inside me."

His tongue flicked her earlobe. "Sweetheart, twenty minutes isn't going to cut it. Hell, twenty *hours* still wouldn't be enough time for me to do all the things I want to do to you."

This man. *God.* He somehow managed to steal her heart,

piece by tiny piece, with his words, his actions . . . just by being him.

Rachel leaned back and took his face in her palms. "Twenty hours sounds painful, quite honestly." When he parted his lips, she kissed away his retort, sliding her tongue into his mouth to tangle with his. Her lungs were threatening to burst by the time she pulled back. "So, now we have eighteen minutes. Let's make the most of them, while we have them, okay?"

His fingers flexed on her arms, cock pulsing beneath her, breath coming in rapid gusts. "You sure?"

She reached for her nightstand and extracted a condom. "Get inside me, Bas." She ripped open the packet with her teeth. "Otherwise, I'm taking matters into my own hands."

One heartbeat, blue-gray eyes locked onto hers. Another and . . . Rachel's back hit the mattress.

Her tank top disappeared, tossed over Bas's shoulder, as she worked on the few buttons he'd managed to do up earlier. Finally, they were opened and she shoved his shirt down his shoulders. He shrugged it off then hesitated, fingers on the waistband of his slacks.

She brushed his hands aside and undid them herself. "I'm sure," she panted. "So fucking sure. Now please, Bas. Inside. Now."

Abandoning his pants at the top of his thighs, Rachel reached for his underwear and freed his cock. "God, yes," she said, wrapping one hand around its hard length. "I've missed you so, so much."

Bas groaned, thrusting into her hand. "Fuck, sweetheart. Don't talk to it like that."

She was too busy stroking her palm up and down the velvet steel to pay much attention. "Like what?"

"Like it's your favorite pet and you can't wait to take him out for a ride."

Her lips twitched and she bit back a giggle. "But what if that's exactly what I want?"

"Noted. He wants that, too, but *this* he also wants to make it good."

"It's *already* good."

Sebastian hissed out a curse as she gripped him tightly. "Insert an amusing quip here later," he said, leaning down to suck one nipple into his mouth, making her melt in pleasure, her grip faltering at least until he released it and cupped her cheek. "Fuck, sweetheart, but your hands on me . . ."

Enough teasing. Enough dancing around. Rachel rolled the condom down his length, loving how he groaned and his cock pulsed in her grip. "It's that good?"

Storm-filled blue eyes met hers. "So fucking good." She tugged, positioning him between her spread thighs, but when she shifted, trying to take him inside, Bas hesitated for a beat. "Are you—?"

Another one of those pieces of her heart slipped from her chest, headed toward Sebastian's hands. Already, he held that and so much more of her. She liked him so, *so* much.

"Twelve minutes," she reminded. "Also, I'm sure. Really, *really* sure." She thrust her hips up and *fuck*. He was big and hard and—

He started moving.

She forgot everything except how good he felt sliding in and out, how he kissed her like she was the most precious thing in the universe, how he slipped one hand between them to press firmly on her clit, how he knew that one touch would send her skyrocketing up and then over the peak into the abyss of blind pleasure down below.

"Fuck, baby," he groaned and thrust once, twice, three more times before he was calling out her name and joining her in the chasm beneath.

"Why did I think twenty minutes was enough time again?"

"Because you're nuts?" Bas said.

Rachel was in the shower while Sebastian stood by the sink. She could feel his gaze scorching her through the clear glass panes and wanted to open the door and invite him in.

But work.

And responsibilities and adulting.

Barf.

She stuck her head under the water, letting it sluice over her body and wet her hair.

Mid-shampoo, a gust of cold inundated her and her eyes flew open on a gasp.

Bas stood outside the shower, that molten stare on her.

"Fuck," he said and closed the door. "Next time, we are so doing it in the shower."

"We could—"

"Woman," he growled. "I'm wise to your ways by now. Don't you dare finish that sentence." Deliberately, he faced away from her and picked up the toothbrush she'd pulled out from her set of unopened spares the previous night.

Rachel's lips twitched.

"Stop smiling."

She smoothed conditioner through her hair. "How do you know I'm smiling?"

This snarly side of him was new, but instead of making her nervous, as she might have half-expected, she actually kind of liked it. Even bad-tempered, Sebastian still looked at her with gentleness in his expression.

"I can feel your smile from here."

"You gave me two of the best orgasms of my life. Clearly, I have something to smile about."

He whirled around, toothbrush in hand. "Only two of the best?"

"Well, you did give me a couple of excellent ones last time we were together."

One side of Bas's mouth quirked up.

"Thought you'd like that," she said.

"Your ego boosts are a thing of beauty."

She smothered a giggle, gave her hair one more rinse, then began soaping up. Sebastian turned back to the sink with a groan. "I've got to get out of here."

Rachel cranked off the water. "I thought you were going to shower."

"I need a cold one at this point."

She pushed open the door and snagged a towel, taking her time in wrapping it around her body, loving the way Bas's eyes never left her body, even though the toothbrush was hanging out of his mouth.

Stopping just in front of him, she ran one finger down his chest. "Spit."

He choked. "What?" It sounded like, "Shmut?"

"Sink. Toothpaste. Spit."

Bas followed her orders, hands clamped into fists.

"Now shower," she told him. "I'm going to get dressed."

"Thank God," he muttered. "For the sake of my sanity, I need you to not be naked—"

She dropped her towel to the tile floor.

Rachel had never heard that particular curse word combination before.

She found that she liked it.

SIXTEEN

Sebastian

HIS TUESDAY HAD CERTAINLY STARTED off right.

Unfortunately, it didn't continue that way.

Sighing at the welcome package waiting outside the Steele building, Bas steeled himself.

At least four reporters stood on the sidewalk in front of the building. Normally, he'd be able to breeze right by them, since he wasn't exactly the face of the business—that was Clay—but Sebastian had been interviewed by one of the reporters recently with regards to the project.

So instead of striding by unnoticed, Samantha's laser gaze caught him the moment he stepped out of the Uber and onto the sidewalk in front of the building.

"Sebastian!" she called, racing over.

Not idiots, the rest of the reporters rushed to join her.

Four cameras pointed in his direction and it was just perfect that he was wearing his wrinkled white button-down and giving off definite one-night stand vibes.

Shit. He started to slip on his jacket, thinking to cover as many of the wrinkles as possible then froze.

Because maybe he could swing this in his favor.

Samantha began walking next to him.

"City officials say that big businesses in San Francisco are sucking up tax breaks and resources, but not giving back as previously agreed. With Steele Technologies withdrawing from the tech and community center project, it's hard to disagree."

Bas rubbed a hand over his face. "That's not a question, Samantha, but you know all of us at Steele Technologies have been working long hours on this project that would bring tech resources to several underserved and very deserving communities." He flashed her a smile. "We discussed this very center less than a month ago."

"So, what's changed?" another reporter asked. "Why back out now?"

Sebastian didn't have to hide his disappointment when answering. "We didn't want to back out, but the city has made it nearly impossible for us to proceed. They've thrown up roadblocks every step along the way. I mean, just look at me. I've been up half the night trying to find a way to move forward."

They chuckled and Samantha indicated her cheeks. "I don't know. The stubble thing is working for you."

"Not likely, but I'm not sure how to proceed at this point." He began ticking off his fingers. "They've required three additional environmental reviews, four different structural engineers to sign off on the drawings, and two extra seismic reports. We want the project to be successful and obviously for the space to be safe for the community, but we've spent almost as much as budgeted for the entire project on pre-construction alone." Bas stopped just before entering the building. "And I don't think that it's a coincidence that the latest contractor we've been required to hire for a quote-un-quote final seismic calculation is the brother-in-law of Councilman Han, do you?"

Samantha smirked, blond ponytail flicking over her shoulder. "I guess we'll find out, Sebastian."

"I hope you do," he said. "We at Steele sincerely want this project to move forward. For now, I've got to get back to work."

The reporters thanked Bas as he opened the door.

Just before it closed behind him, Samantha caught it and asked, "Any chance you can score me playoff tickets? I heard your brother has a box at the Gold Mine."

"Wait," one of the other reporters, a male with a horrible goatee and slightly pudgy middle, asked. "Your brother is *the* Devon Scott?"

Samantha nodded.

"I second the request for tickets. The Gold actually have a real shot at the Cup this year."

Bas mentally sighed. Even though he'd been retired for close to five years now, the mystique of Devon Scott lived on.

"No hookup on my end," he said. "Sorry."

And with a brisk wave, he took off for the elevators.

SEBASTIAN HUNG up the phone after speaking with Clay in depth about the tech center. Sighing, he leaned back in his office chair. He hadn't wanted to call his boss, had hoped to avoid the conversation altogether and perhaps just share the events of the fallout from the tech center when Clay returned from Berlin as a funny addendum to an otherwise uneventful trip.

But, unfortunately, that was not to be.

With the media on the trail and potentially two huge businesses—RoboTech and Steele Technologies—in their crossfire, Bas had done the prudent thing and filled in his boss.

Clay had taken it surprisingly well, pulling Heather on to speakerphone and the two of them beginning to brainstorm both a solution to the city's roadblocks and some additional ways to get the press on their side.

Clearly, both he and his wife were not good at the relaxation thing.

Heather, apparently, had walked out of the two-hour massage Clay had booked her because, "Who could sit still for that long, anyway?"

"Crazy kids," he muttered, though he was feeling more than a little jealous that Clay had found someone so perfect for him.

Not that he could begrudge his boss. He just wanted to be there with Rachel.

Patience.

They'd already come leaps and bounds and it hadn't even been a week.

And plus, with Clay taking the tech center off his plate, now Sebastian had a bit more free time to win Rachel over.

Time to bust out his wooing skills.

Snorting at his own idiocy, Bas began making a list of everything he wanted to do for Rachel. Flowers, obviously, and he needed to find out which type was her favorite. A nice dinner or *dinners*. Luckily, San Francisco had plenty of incredible restaurants, and she'd picked up Italian for them the previous night, so a trip down to Little Italy was definitely on the books. He also needed to figure out if she liked hockey, because despite his lie to Samantha, the reporter, Devon *did* have a box at the Gold Mine, so NHL games were definitely on the docket if Rachel enjoyed that sort of thing.

He wondered if there were any concerts coming up.

Bas certainly wouldn't mind spending the night cuddled next to her as she danced to her favorite songs.

Hell, he was so gone for her already that he could picture

the smile on her face and the joy in her eyes as she listened and he wouldn't even care if it was some hideous boy band or pop duo. Bas would do whatever it took to make her happy.

Sap, he imagined Kelsey saying.

Damn straight, he was.

Rachel was special, and he intended to treat her that way.

Okay, so flowers and—oh—chocolates. Dinner and some nights out. What else? A documentary showing?

He opened his inbox. He could have sworn that he'd gotten an email inviting him to a film festival recently—

The knock at the door interrupted his searching.

His assistant—yes, hilariously or not, he had an assistant as the . . . assistant. Puns or not, Keiran waited for Bas to tell him to come in then opened the door and stuck his head through the gap. "There's a delivery for you."

Awesome. He'd been waiting on several boxes of files. "Thanks, Key. Just put them on the table."

Keiran nodded and disappeared then came back into Bas's office with full hands . . . they just weren't full of what he'd expected. Instead of files, Keiran carried a black garment bag, a small silver bag from a well-known men's clothing store, and a medium-sized box.

"Uh." Bas shook himself. "Thanks, Keiran. I'll let you know if I need anything else."

His assistant left with a nod and shut the door behind him.

"What the hell?" Sebastian muttered, pushing up from his chair and walking over to the conference table that took up one half of his office.

He unzipped the garment bag first. Inside was a suit identical to the one he was wearing, except it was made from a fabric he'd never seen in the store before. Bas might drive a Toyota, but he didn't skimp on his suits. Hell, half his luxury car budget had probably gone into his closet.

Those suits were also pretty much the single thing he did to follow in his brother's footsteps. As in, he went to the same small tailor that Devon had and still frequented. It was in the South Bay and the suits that came out of that little shop were as good as any luxury store. Cost about as much, too, but Devon and later Bas both swore by them.

It had only taken purchasing one suit from somewhere else —and a really long day spent pulling at the inseam, trying to adjust the too-tight shoulders, attempting to ignore the itchy waistband—for Sebastian to realize the error of his ways.

He didn't buy anywhere else now.

Even Clay had started ordering his suits from the same shop.

And since he hadn't ordered a new suit, the person who'd sent it obviously knew and understood Bas's obsession.

It was the exact suit he favored, just in a pattern he'd never seen and probably would have never ordered for himself. An almost navy blue with a subtle brown pinstripe, the fabric was different and . . . it was awesome.

As were the soft blue tie and the crisp white button-down.

He also still didn't know who'd sent it.

Bas slipped the suit from the garment bag and hung it on the back of his door.

That was when he saw the note.

The cream envelope had his name scribbled on the front and for a second, Sebastian thought that perhaps Clay had sent the suit as a thank you or a bonus. But the note wasn't from his boss.

Bas,
Heather always keeps an extra suit in her office for just
these circumstances. I did some snooping while you were
in the shower. Hope you like this one.

-*Rach*

P.S. I like the stubble look as well. It goes with what's in the bag. (You'll see.) Let me know if you're free tonight so we can get lumbersexual.

Lumbersexual?

"What the—?" He shook his head and opened the bag. Jeans and a red plaid flannel shirt were inside, along with a pair of boots that were probably way too cool for him, but he'd rock them anyway.

Another note was stuck in one boot.

If you're free tonight . . . we get to use what's in the box.

Okay, so Sebastian could get behind the sound of that.

Then he opened the lid.

An ax was inside.

Uhhh . . .

He lifted it up, holding it by the handle. It was surprisingly light and since he felt like he could reasonably assume that Rachel didn't want to go on an ax-murdering spree . . . and that this little dinky ax wouldn't be of much use for that anyway. . .

Thankfully, before his mind could go further down that particular stretch, Bas's phone rang.

Still holding the ax, he answered it without looking at the screen. "Sebastian speaking."

"I thought you liked Bas."

Rachel's voice immediately made a smile break out on his face. "Hey, sweetheart," he said.

"Hi." Her tone had gentled. "I have to admit, and will probably need to turn in my feminist card for it, but I like it when you call me sweetheart."

His smile widened. "I'm glad."

"So," she said, now almost brusquely. "I'm guessing you've gotten my present by now?"

"They're amazing," he replied. Well, the ax was confusing, but the suit and clothes were incredible. "It's way too much, sweetheart. You really shouldn't have done that."

"It's my fault that you were caught out in the media in a disgracefully wrinkled suit."

He snorted. "Worth it." A beat. "Plus, your idea is brilliant. I'm going to start making sure that Clay has an extra suit in his office, just in case."

"And you," she said.

"And me," he agreed. "But I did have a question about—"

"Lumbersexual or the ax?"

Bas laughed. "Either. Both."

"I am woman, hear me roar. I can throw an ax like Thor."

He leaned against the table. "Um, I hate to ruin your rhyme, but Thor actually has a hammer."

"Details, details. But"—she hesitated and Sebastian's heart pulsed when her voice went tentative—"I just thought it might be fun to try that ax throwing thing?"

Ax throwing?

"I—"

"It's stupid, I know. But there's this place outside the city where you can like go throw axes at a target. You like rent a lane for an hour. There's food and beer and—" She broke off. "Never mind. This was a stupid idea."

"Rachel."

"Forget I said anything." Her breath rattled through the speaker on his phone. "And for God's sake, forget about the ax. Just forget—"

"*Rachel.*"

She stopped talking.

"Do you know what I was doing before your way too generous delivery appeared in my office?"

"No," she squeaked.

"I was planning all the ways I wanted to romance and seduce you."

"*Oh.*"

"Yes," he said. "I had dinner and flowers—what's your favorite kind, by the way?"

"Tulips," she said, almost shyly. "Yellow, if you can find them."

"Yellow tulips," he repeated. "Got it. But back to me and you for a moment. Before your package came, I'd been making a list of all the things I wanted to do for you."

"For me?" she asked. "Not to?"

He smirked. "Well, the things I want to do to you are obvious, yeah? I was trying to plan some dates to win you over and make you actually like me."

She giggled. "I already *do* like you."

"Well, that's a relief."

"So . . ." Rachel trailed off.

"So, I'd love to go chuck some axes with you."

"And you'll wear the flannel?"

"Do lumberjacks turn you on?" he asked, thinking of all the ways he could work that angle.

"Sure. But I just really want to see you not in a suit."

"Sweetheart, does this morning not count? Or were you just not paying attention?"

"Oh, I was paying attention, but flannel is sexy."

"Along with throwing axes."

He could feel her shrug. "Yup."

"Okay. Should I meet you there or pick you up?"

If she was surprised by his agreement, Rachel didn't let on. Instead, they spent a few minutes working out details before he hung up with a promise from her to not buy him any more presents.

He had a hell of a lot to make up for on that front.

Here he'd been thinking of all the ways to romance her, and she'd wooed him in return.

Wooed?

Hell, that should have made him feel emasculated, right? But Bas couldn't find that particular feeling within him. Rather, he was touched that she'd done something so thoughtful and kind without expecting anything in return.

It was all too much, but it was also certainly the nicest thing that anyone had ever done for him.

Which made him want to do the same for her.

Sebastian pulled up his text messages, scrolled down to the chain he had going with his boss, and figured what the hell did he have to lose at this point? He wasn't going to hide his feelings for Rachel. Not when she was so important.

Not work related, but can you pick Heather's brain for me? I want to get Rachel something really special that she wouldn't buy for herself.

Clay's reply came less than a minute later.

It's like that, is it?

Yes, it was. He liked Rachel—so damned much.

It's like that. And also so much more.

A minute of silence that almost killed him then Clay wrote back.

According to Heather, these.

Clay attached a link. Another buzz came before Sebastian could open it.

My wife also says that if you hurt Rachel, she will personally disembowel you.

Bas didn't have a problem with that.

If I do hurt Rachel, I'll stand still and let Heather do it.

A moment passed before:

I was going to tell you not to ruin the perfect duo Heather and I had set up to run the world, but I don't think I need to. Be open. Trust yourself. And just love her as she deserves to be loved.

Love her?
Did he?
Could he?
But how could he *not?*
Clay sent another message.

Fuck me, that was deep. But seriously, Sebastian—work less and play more.

Despite the truth circling in his brain, the obvious, yet somehow still shocking truth, Sebastian managed to find his voice.

Pot meet kettle.

Clay's final message made Bas snort.

Let's work on it together.

And he attached a video of two pigeons tag-teaming the thievery of a bag of potato chips . . . from inside a very busy store.

See, I'm working less and wasting all sorts of time on social media now.

Sebastian thought that the less work thing might actually be working for his boss.

It had found him a woman he wanted to spend the rest of his life with, after all.

And that sounded pretty damned good.

Bas opened the link and started shopping.

SEVENTEEN

Rachel

OKAY, jokes aside, the lumbersexual thing really *did* do it for her.

Rachel was seriously enjoying the view of the flannel tightening over Bas's shoulders as he lifted his arms to throw the ax.

That *thunking* sound of it hitting and sinking into the wood was hot, too.

Very manly and masculine and—

"Are you looking at my butt?" Bas asked, turning around and catching her in her obvious appraisal. His eyes twinkled in amusement.

She crossed her arms. "Yeah? And so what if I was?"

"I would say, I've been checking out your ass, too."

He smirked when her cheeks went pink then turned and made a show of bending to pick up his final ax, taking his time to aim and throw. It hit the target but didn't actually stick into the wood, just a few inches left of the bull's-eye.

Ax throwing, she'd found out, was harder than she'd expected.

Just throw a sharp object at some wood, it couldn't be that tough.

Ha.

She'd ended up missing the target completely, hitting with the wrong side of the ax totally, or not throwing it hard enough for it to bury itself in the wood.

But after her third turn, she'd started to get the hang of it, and it was actually really fun.

Or maybe that was being with Sebastian.

He had shrugged when the ax fell and walked forward to collect them from the target and the floor. He set them on the counter at the front of the lane then picked up his beer and settled next to her on the bench she was watching from.

"How's yours?" he asked, pointing at her beer. "Apricot, right?"

Rachel smiled. "Normally, I'd make fun of someone ordering a fruity beer like this, but Sera actually got me hooked on this brand."

"Really? Seraphina likes beer?" he asked and winced. "Sorry. It's just she seems so—"

"Barbie-like?"

Sebastian made a face. "I—uh—"

Rachel laughed. "It's fine. Plus, Sera would be the first to tell you that she resembles the blond-haired, pink-adorned doll, but the similarities end on the surface. She's a beer-drinking, sports-watching woman . . . who also happens to adore romance novels and *Desperate Housewives*."

"That's an *interesting* combination."

Rachel grinned at him. "What can I say? I love all those things, too. Well, I'm a huge fan of hockey and definitely love television dramas and romance novels. And I don't mind a beer here or there, but I mostly prefer wine." She laughed. "Anyway,

I really need to shut up now, because this has to seriously be the most boring conversation ever."

Bas's voice went almost hard. "*Never* shut up. I love hearing you talk."

Her brows lifted. "You seriously want to hear me expound on television dramas."

Blue-gray irises met hers. "Sweetheart, I want to hear *anything* you have to say."

Aw. This man. Seriously. Just. This. Man.

She cupped his cheek, sliding closer to stare deeply into his eyes. "Okay," she murmured. "I won't shut up." A beat. "Also, how do you feel about curly fries?"

Bas tipped his face down to kiss the tip of her nose. "I think curly fries sound awesome. I'll order them." He stood and tugged her to her feet. "Now, go throw some axes so I can watch my sexy girl's ass."

His girl.

Yeah. She could get used to that.

———

DESPITE HER ATTEMPTS for the opposite, Sebastian left her at her door that evening.

"I'm trying to date you, woman," he grumbled when she'd tugged him inside her apartment and all but jumped into his arms. "Not get in your pants."

Worth it though, especially when he turned to pin her against the door and kissed the ever-loving sense out of her.

"But what if I want you in my pants?" she'd asked and had been thrilled when he'd groaned and dropped his forehead to the panel.

"Killing me, sweetheart."

"I think you're sexy," she'd said and been rewarded with another kiss.

But then he really had left.

And taken her heart with him.

How in the hell could a woman like her, with a past like hers, with a track record for the people she'd trusted . . . how could she have fallen in love so quickly?

She should be cautious, should be protecting herself, should be running and screaming in the other direction.

Except, she had learned to trust over the last year and a half. Rachel had made friends who supported her, who had invited her into their hearts and opened their arms to hold her tight, to help wrench her from her past.

They helped her see that there were good people, good *men* in the world.

And she *knew* that Sebastian was so, so different from Preston.

But she also knew that she was in way over her head with Bas and bound to make a mess of this.

She'd pulled out her laptop.

It was time to muster the resources of the Sextant.

Heather, despite the late hour in Berlin, was the first to answer the call. "I just knew you were going to call me," she said. "Oh my God. I've been gone all of four days, what the hell is going on with my unflappable assistant?"

"I—"

Abby logged on, baby Emma sound asleep on one shoulder. "Non-book club video-chat session," she crowed. "All the drama. Heather, what did you do now? You'd better not be divorcing Clay *again*, I don't care if he—"

"Abby," Heather interrupted. "Rachel made the call."

"What?" Abby froze, but as always managed to recover

herself quickly. Hazel eyes pinned Rachel in place through the laptop screen. "You. Drama. Dish. Now."

Bec's face appeared midway through that declaration. "Did having all those babies scramble your use of the English language?"

Abby smirked. "Probably." She bent to kiss Emma's head. "But still worth it."

Bec pretended to puke, but she was smiling. "What'd you do now, Heather?"

Heather threw her hands up. "I didn't *do* anything! Why does everyone keep asking that?"

Clay's head popped into the frame of Heather's camera as he kissed her on the cheek. He looked extra yummy in his workout clothes. "I'm out of here." He turned to wave at them. "For the record, she did do something . . . or rather *someone*."

CeCe and Sera appeared almost simultaneously, catching the tail end of Clay's statement, as well as the pillow Heather launched in his direction as he sauntered off.

And silence.

CeCe opened her mouth—

"It wasn't me," Heather snapped and pointed at her camera. "It's the quiet, steady one."

All eyes turned to Rachel's face on the screen.

She couldn't feel it considering her friends were miles to oceans apart, but she still knew all their attention was focused on her.

Which nearly made her chicken out.

But, no, dammit, she thought, lifting her chin and straightening her shoulders. She was going to do the normal—okay, *semi*-normal—well-adjusted thing. She was . . .

"I slept with Sebastian."

Going to blurt it all out, apparently.

"Well," she scrambled. "I mean, I slept with him like three

months ago. You know that night some of us met up at Bobby's. I —uh—didn't go home early. I kind of took him back to the hotel room I had been staying at while my apartment was being renovated and then I—*we*—"

"Banged like two teenagers on prom night?" Sera supplied.

Rachel winced. "Um, kind of?"

"Word of advice, kid," Bec said. "Stop trying to be hip. You had sex with Sebastian three months back and go." She gestured for Rachel to continue talking.

"Well, he kind of ditched me while I was in the shower. I came out and he'd gone."

Outraged gasps exploded out of her speakers.

"No," she hurried to say. "That's not the issue. There was a problem at work. He had to go and I've left—" She waved a hand. "Regardless, we didn't exactly exchange information . . . or even names—"

Five voices began talking almost at once.

"You exchanged *something*," CeCe muttered.

"Holy shit," from Abby who promptly covered baby Emma's ears and repeated. "Holy fucking shit."

"No names?" Bec grinned. "I told you to get un-virginized, but damn girl, I'm impressed."

"That sounds kind of dangerous," Sera said. "Bringing a strange man back to your hotel room." To which Abby winced and started protesting that she'd met Jordan in that exact same way.

Heather raised her fist to the screen. "Nice work. Honestly, I didn't know you had it in you, kid."

"Guys!" Rachel cried and threw up her hands. "The one-night stand was . . ."

"Outstanding?" Bec asked. "Or at least, that's what you told me."

Abby gasped. "You told her first?"

"Oh my God," Rachel dropped her head into her hands. "Yes, it was good. *Really* fucking good, but that night isn't the point. Well, neither is this morning, I guess. It's—"

"This *morning*?" Heather repeated.

CeCe hooted. Bec and Abby grinned.

"Why did I call you all again?"

"Because you love us," Sera said. "Okay, obviously, you like him or you wouldn't have slept with him again. So, what's the real problem?"

"Is it because he works for Clay?" Heather asked. "You know, if it's important to you, we'll find a way to make it work. I want to keep you around, Rach. I honestly don't think I could do this without you."

"This, *what*?" CeCe teased. "Running your own life? Or keeping your workaholic side busy enough?"

Heather snorted. "Yes, to both."

Rachel shook her head. "It's not because he works for Clay," she said. "But thank you for being open to figuring it out. It—" And dammit, her eyes filled with tears. "It's—" A sniff. "Shit. It's because before I started working for you, Heather, my life was a fucking mess."

And then she told her friends everything.

She told them about her mom leaving, her dad and the way he used to smack her around when she'd made him angry, her grandparents and their sharp, controlling words. Then finally, she told them about Preston and his heavy fists, the blows to her body, the way he'd controlled every aspect of her life, from the food she ate to who she spent time with to the pleasure or pain she received in bed.

"I don't know how I managed to land the job with you, Heather," she said, wiping her eyes on the hem of her T-shirt. "My résumé was a mess and I hardly had any work experience at all. Plus, I felt like I was in a fog during that whole interview."

Heather shrugged. "I'll admit that you *were* lacking on the experience front, but, Rachel, there was something about you that was so determined I couldn't help but offer you the job. I wanted to see that spark inside you grow."

"Don't start up the waterworks again," Rachel said and sniffed. "But, whatever the reason you picked me, I can't thank you enough."

"Shit!" Bec's outburst drew all their gazes. She narrowed her eyes at them. "I don't have any tissues and—"

"Oh, no," Abby cried. "Are you not using that waterproof mascara?"

CeCe shook her head. "You know, you used to be a normal person who didn't worry about mascara and its waterproof qualities."

"I *used* to be a normal person before these kids rotted my brains."

"Brains?" Sera teased. "As in more than one?"

"Ugh." Abby sighed and flopped back onto the bed she was perched on. "You guys are seriously the worst."

"You love us," Heather said.

"Also, let it be noted that I wasn't complaining about my mascara at all," Bec said. "Rather that you bitches are making me have all these . . ."

"Feelings?" CeCe said with a smirk.

"Yes. Those." Bec grinned. "Pesky little things." She clapped her hands together. "I've got the Preston asshole tied up legally in a dozen different ways, and his daddy's district attorney's connection will quickly be coming to an end. As for the rest of it—"

"The feelings part?" Sera asked.

"Yes. *That*," Bec replied. "You lot had better help her. I've done all I can."

Rachel shook her head, biting back her smile. "I thought you gave me excellent advice when I talked to you about Bas."

"One time lucky girl talk session." Bec shrugged. "You need me to sue him, I'm your girl."

"I would like it noted that I feel like *I* should have been the go-to girl for Sebastian talk," Heather said.

Abby beat Rachel to her explanation. "Honeymoon."

"Pish." Heather rolled her eyes. "Plus, I'm going insane," she whined. "This is the least busy I've been on a trip in probably a decade. What am I supposed to do?"

"I don't know, *your husband*," CeCe said.

Abby cackled.

Well, okay they all did.

"Yes, yes," Heather muttered. "Clay is taking care of me in that department, but I'm bored."

"You're also taking over," Sera said.

Heather froze. "Damn. I am. Sorry, Rach."

"First, you've had three business meetings in the last two days, so still working," Rachel said. "Second. Take over all you want. I'm fine."

"If you were fine, you wouldn't have called us," Bec pointed out.

Rather unhelpfully, Rachel thought, leaning back against her couch cushions and sighing. "Okay, be logical, why don't you? I know I'm not fine, but I also—*fuck*, I don't know I *am* fine."

"Explain, please," Heather said.

"Like I feel a lot for Bas, too much for such a short time, but also like just the right amount. My gut is like this is great, he's so perfect and amazing and a little dorky and he writes me poems and actually cares about me . . ."

"He writes poems?" CeCe asked.

"Focus," Bec told them. "Poem talk later. Revelations now."

"Who's the caveman now?" Abby muttered.

Rachel laughed then sighed. "You guys. I'm so messed up. I thought it would take me forever to just trust another man to *kiss* me. Then I jumped into bed with Sebastian and it was so incredible and even this morning, he wanted to wait, to give me more time, but I was the one who really wanted to go for it."

"And?"

She didn't know which of her friends had asked that. She was too deep in her internal quagmire of thoughts that it merely spurred her on.

"All I know," she said. "Is that sex aside, when I close my eyes and picture a random day in the future—a month, a year, *more*—I see Bas with me."

"Isn't that enough for now?" CeCe asked.

"But what if I panic a month from now?" she said. "What if I'm fine now, but it's all a strange coping mechanism and then I'm going to freak out down the line?"

"Newsflash, kid," Heather said. "We *all* have freak outs."

"Right," Abby added. "Plus, if and when you do freak out, you and Sebastian will either get through it or you'll know then it wasn't meant to be."

"But what if—"

"Do you really need to have *all* the answers now?" Sera asked. "Or are you just looking for a convenient excuse to pull away?"

Fuck.

"Oh my God," Rachel said. "You guys are good." She scrubbed a hand over her face and straightened. "So, I'm doing this?"

Bec fixed her with a glance. "You tell us."

Rachel bit her lip, sighed, and then straightened her shoulders and pushed the final tendrils of her past deep down.

"I am *so* doing this."

EIGHTEEN

Sebastian

IT WAS Thursday and instead of heading over to Rachel's office to coax her away from work and talk her into dinner at his place, he was walking into a very nice, expensive restaurant near the waterfront.

Sighing, he handed off his coat to the hostess but declined her offer to take him to the table.

He could already see his family.

Bas was having Rachel withdrawals. They'd texted constantly over the last two days, sent a few business-related emails. They'd even had plans last night.

But Rachel had to cancel because a work meeting in Los Angeles ran long and she hadn't gotten back into the city until after eleven o'clock that night.

All logical reasons.

He still was almost desperate to wrap her in his arms and just smell—

Just smell her?

Fuck, he was losing it.

His phone buzzed and he pulled it out, half-expecting it to be Kelsey, telling him to get his ass in gear.

Instead, it was Rachel.

I just finished. Want to grab foods?

Foods? She was too cute. And yes. Yes, he did want to grab *foods*.

Unfortunately, he could not. But she sent another text before he could reply.

Oh shoot, I'm losing my mind. I just remembered that you're having dinner with your family and now I'm probably interrupting. Ugh. Sorry! Talk to you later.

She was fucking adorable.

He was just typing out a response to tell her that when his phone was snatched out of his hands.

"Stop working to avoid us, bro," Kelsey said.

"It's not—"

Which was pretty much the worst thing he could have said because then Kelsey glanced down at the screen and a wide smile broke out across her face. "Who's Rachel?"

"Shut up." He reached for his phone as his sister scrolled up.

"Holy shit," she said, eyes wide. "Those are either seriously dangerous HR violations or Sebastian has a *girlfriend*."

Considering she all but sang the last and held his cell out of his reach, Bas was ready to kill his sister . . . or at least tackle her to the ground and tear the phone from her cold, limp fingers.

Especially when she pressed a button on the screen.

She wasn't.

She seriously. Was. Not.

Except, she *was*. Kelsey put the phone to her ear. "Hi, is this Rachel? This is Kelsey, Sebastian's sister. Oh no, don't apologize, you're not interrupting. I just wanted to invite you to join us." A pause as she listened for all of two seconds then began talking again. "*No*. You wouldn't be intruding. Sebastian has told us so much about you. Please, come."

Kill him now.

Kelsey began walking toward the table his family occupied. Bas moved after her a beat later, but he wasn't far enough to miss her exclaim, "Great! I'm so excited to meet you."

She stopped in her tracks, so quickly that he almost mowed her down, and hung up, turning to slam the cell into his chest.

Then she hot-footed it over to the table where his parents, Devon, and his wife, Becca, sat and declared, "Sebastian's girlfriend is joining us for dinner!"

He was going to kill her.

IN SHORT ORDER, another chair was pulled over and Sebastian was being inundated with questions.

"How did you meet her?" Devon asked.

"What's she like?" From his dad.

"It's been so long since you've brought a girl home!" His mom's gleeful exclamation.

Thankfully, his phone buzzed, granting him a reprieve.

I'm on my way, but I definitely don't have to be.

If Rachel didn't already own his heart, that text would have done the trick.

"Aw," Becca murmured, snapping him out of his thoughts. "Look at his face. He *really* does like her."

Shaking his head, he typed out a response.

Please come and save me from the evil that is my sister.

Of course, Kelsey happened to glance over his shoulder as he sent that. "Ouch," she said. "That's mean."

"Bad things happen to people who stick their noses into other people's business," he gritted out.

Kelsey smiled. "If I didn't push, you'd just isolate yourself even more."

"Hard to isolate yourself from something you're not even part of."

She frowned. "What the hell does *that* mean?"

Fortunately, the server came at that moment to take their drink order and they put in for a couple of appetizers. Becca "awed" again when he asked for a glass of red wine for Rachel.

They'd just finished the order of Oysters Rockefeller when Rachel walked into the restaurant.

He was standing and walking toward her before he even realized that he'd moved.

And fuck, but her smile at his approach just took his breath away.

She looked a little frazzled, her hair a little windblown and her coat tied haphazardly, but she was beautiful and fuck did he love her.

"Hi," she murmured.

He crouched a little to draw her gaze when she looked around nervously. "Hey, you." Brown eyes met his and she visibly relaxed.

"Hi, sorry," she said. "I'm unreasonably nervous about meeting your family."

"They're a lot, but they mean well," he told her. "Feel free to run at any point. I'll make your excuses."

She released a shuddering breath and nodded. "Sounds like a plan."

"Come on. I'll introduce you." He handed off her coat to the hostess with a murmured thanks then slipped his arm through hers and led her to the table.

His family stood as they approached.

"Rachel," Devon said. "It's so nice to meet you. This is my wife, Becca."

She shook both their hands then extended her palm to his mom and dad. "Hi, Mr. and Mrs. Scott. I hope you don't mind me intruding on your dinner."

"Oh, not at all," his mom said. "We're happy we've had a chance to meet you. Sebastian can rarely join us for dinner when we're in town."

"He works really hard," Rachel said and turned to his sister. "Kelsey?"

"In the flesh," his sister joked. "I'm glad you came."

Rachel's lips twitched as they all took a seat. "I'm not sure I had much of a choice," she said. "But I am honored to be included."

They settled into their drinks as a few more appetizers were ordered after Bas's mom had given Rachel the fifth degree about her food preferences. Then she polled Bas, Devon, Becca, and Kelsey as if she didn't already know whether they preferred calamari or shrimp cocktail.

His mother knew all—she just wanted everyone to feel included.

Or so she claimed.

If that were the case, then why had he always been the odd man out?

Why had they never come to his school events? Or sports games? Or—

He was way too old to be holding a grudge about childhood

insecurities. His parents had done the best they could. They'd made mistakes as all parents did, of course, but he'd had food and love and—

He'd always felt left out.

Boo hoo, Scott, he sneered at himself. *You're a grown man. Get over it.*

Rachel slid her hand into his. "You okay?" she asked softly.

"I'm—"

"So," his dad said, "how did you two meet?"

Sebastian inwardly groaned, just waiting for the jokes.

But Rachel smiled and suddenly all those old hurts from his childhood didn't matter. Not when he had her and she was smiling at him like he was important.

"Funny story, actually," she said. "Bas and I met because our bosses fell in love and got married."

"Aw," Becca said and sniffed. When all eyes turned to her, she turned beet red. "Oh gosh, I'm sorry. That's just so sweet, and Devon and I met when we—"

Tears streaked down her cheeks.

Rachel looked alarmed. "I—uh—sorry if I offended—"

"No." Becca wiped her eyes on her napkin. "I'm just a mess because I'm pregnant!"

Kelsey jumped to her feet and rounded the table. "Holy shit, that's amazing! I thought the doctor said that the IVF might take a long time to—" She shook her head. "Never mind. How far along are you?"

"IVF?"

Bas didn't realize he'd spoken aloud until Devon winced. "We've been struggling for a while to get pregnant—"

The rest of the words were cut off as his dad swept Devon up into a tight hug that lifted even the six-foot-plus former hockey player off his feet. "I'm going to be a grandpa!"

"Did you know—?" Rachel began.

Sebastian shook his head, wondering what else he'd missed out on knowing since he'd kept his distance over the last years.

Something else also occurred to him.

Something more grim and decidedly much more unpleasant.

How much of his resentment toward his family was truly because he'd been excluded?

And how much was because he'd just done a really good job at pushing them away?

NINETEEN

Rachel

THE PACKAGE WAS WAITING on her desk Friday morning.

Just the symbol on the outside of the box made her breath catch. How could he have possibly known?

But she forgot all about wondering how he'd discovered her obsession when she untied the ribbon.

"Oh my," she sighed.

Inside were two pairs of her favorite—and ridiculously expensive—pajamas. They were folded neatly and wrapped in silky silver tissue paper. She rubbed the material between her thumb and forefinger, beyond touched.

Then her phone buzzed.

Do you like them?

She snatched it up.

Thank you. The pajamas are gorgeous.

A beat, then:

What about the rest? I wasn't sure if you'd like the color .
. .

The rest? Rachel lifted the pajamas from the box and gasped. The first thing she saw was a gorgeous purple robe. It wasn't velvet, but the material was just as soft, and beneath that was . . . a set of lingerie.

An eye-catching amethyst color, the lace set was pretty much the most beautiful set of underwear she'd ever seen.

It was also transparent and—she held up the thong—lacking in material. Smiling, she replied with:

Have plans, do you?

A buzz.

I may have seen it and then pictured a few things.

Rachel snorted.

Little things?

He replied with a GIF of a toddler plunking her hands on her hips and frowning, and Rachel laughed out loud.

Sorry. Big things. Huge things—

Her phone buzzed mid-text.

Do you really like them?

The hint of insecurity made her heart pulse. She'd seen the way he'd put up a good front with his family, but it had to be really hard being the middle sibling of the Scott trio. Older brother is model gorgeous and a professional hockey player, before retiring and starting the most prestigious athlete management company in the States . . . and abroad for that matter. Quite literally, Devon's company was named Prestige Media Group and represented more than a handful of the most popular athletes in the U.S. and abroad. And then there was Kelsey, also beautiful and young and brilliant. She'd called them all together because she'd managed to secure a government contract for her newest project and wanted to celebrate.

Add in Becca's pregnancy news and well, it wasn't surprising that Bas might be feeling the teeniest bit insecure.

Especially since it seemed as though he'd spent a lot of his early years in much the same pattern. His path had been normal —college, working his way through the ranks of a company— while his siblings' paths had been nothing short of exceptional.

Which made it sound as though she thought Sebastian was boring or ordinary.

No, he was incredible.

And while he projected a cool confidence, Rachel wondered how much of that was armor to protect his vulnerable underbelly, to prove to himself and the rest of the world that he was fine on his own, dammit.

But instead of saying any of that, she made a mental promise to make it clear to Bas at some point that regardless of the rest of the world, *she* thought *he* was special.

He was everything.

He was *hers*.

Her fingers flew across the keyboard.

I love them. Thank you, Bas. So much.

His sent an "aw shucks" GIF and she replied with a heart one in turn, and pretty soon she was giggling as they played Gif War by sending increasingly ridiculous images to one another.

Five minutes later, she still hadn't done any work.

But her cheeks hurt from smiling so much.

Yeah, Sebastian was pretty fucking extraordinary as far as she was concerned.

A WEEK LATER, she pushed open her apartment door then immediately stepped out of her heels.

"Thank God," she muttered, kicking them to the side before bending to rub her aching toes. They might be expensive, but the hefty price tag did absolutely nothing for her comfort.

Torture devices, every one of them.

But she didn't need the heels anymore. She was swapping her stilettos for sneakers, her tight business suit for a Gold jersey.

Of course, by the time she made it down to meet Bas, Devon, and Becca at the Gold Mine, she was going to be ridiculously late. Still, she'd never been to a game in a luxury box, and when Sebastian had texted her earlier that day to invite her, she jumped at the opportunity.

Those boxes had free food, right?

Which wasn't the most important part. And also, *boo*, because she'd found out that, no, the food wasn't free. However, she *was* feeling encouraged that Bas might have hit a turning point with his family.

Neither of them had discussed the dinner where his siblings had both shared huge news, but he had mentioned that he was going to try to see them more.

Rachel considered that a step in the right direction.

She was also glad that she hadn't had to badger him into the decision.

She wanted Bas to be proud of himself, not constantly comparing his path with that of his siblings.

But if she had learned anything since leaving Iowa, it was that a person couldn't find their self-worth in others. They could find friends, people to love who shored them up, who supported them when they faltered.

But that deep down worth?

That came from inside.

Yup, she'd learned that firsthand.

And so now, she'd do what she could to encourage Bas to discover his own.

Nodding at herself in the mirror, Rachel ran a quick brush through her hair and touched up her makeup. Windblown—wind-*tornadoed*—wasn't the look she was going for.

She was almost ready to leave when she thought of the box of pretty things Bas had bought for her.

They'd spent a few nights together over the last week, but it had mostly been squeezing in a dinner here or a movie there and she hadn't had the chance to *really* dress up for him.

Or, undress, if she was being truthful

The one time she'd been able to seduce him aside, he'd been sticking very firmly to his slow and steady wooing process.

It was working.

Plus, the crafty bugger had managed to keep them in public places.

Probably because he knew that the moment they were in the privacy of one of their apartments, Rachel would strip herself naked and launch herself at him again.

She was beyond pent up.

Le sigh.

So, the sexy lingerie had been staying in the box.

But . . . she bit her lip.

She was late already, how would five minutes more hurt?

As quickly as she could, she stripped down and swapped her underthings for the gorgeous amethyst lace. And, fuck, if they weren't a perfect fit.

The deep V of the bra somehow enhanced her boobs—what pathetically little of them she had, anyway—and the panties . . . well, they were practically nonexistent, but they still managed to make her lower half look both flat and curvy in all the appropriate places.

And her ass?

She smirked as she turned to view her reflection in the bathroom mirror.

Oh yeah, Bas was going to like that. A whole hell of a lot.

Jeans and sneakers went back on, followed by her long-sleeved tee and her jersey. Just wearing the lingerie made her feel different. Hell, even her clothes fit differently, and she was getting definite naughty vibes when skin that wasn't normally exposed to the elements, so to speak, met the slight rough of denim. Even her breasts were a little va-va-voom under the jersey.

Yup, Bas was definitely going to be happy with her surprise.

Grabbing her purse and cell off the counter, she hurried to the front door.

She was so excited to meet Sebastian that she didn't notice her heels.

She'd kicked them off immediately upon entering her apartment, leaving them to lie haphazardly near her front door.

But by the time she stepped into the hall, they'd been straightened—a pair of twin soldiers perched neatly on her shoe rack.

TWENTY

Sebastian

DEVON AND BECCA were sickeningly in love.

It was disgusting.

Truly revolting.

Bas only hoped that he and Rachel would be the same way.

This was the first time that Bas had been in Devon's box, and he had to admit that he hadn't even thought about coming with or asking for tickets until Samantha, the reporter, had joked about it and Rachel had mentioned that she'd liked hockey.

He liked hockey himself, had always rooted for Devon from the comfort of his own home or when dragged to the arena by his family. But he'd never asked his brother for tickets because . . .

He sighed.

Because it was strings. Another way he couldn't compete.

Juvenile.

As in, he'd been a juvenile.

He'd never begrudged his brother his success. Or his sister

for that matter, but he'd always felt this sense of disappointment from his family.

Why wasn't he special? Why didn't he live up to the Scott legacy?

Which was, frankly, ridiculous. His dad ran a feed store. His mom stayed at home. They were normal middle-class Americans. So where in the fuck had this pressure to be great come from?

From himself.

He sighed again.

From being competitive and distant when his siblings had never been.

Becca stood up and slipped out of the suite, breezily saying something about stretching her legs.

But Bas quickly realized it had been a ploy.

Because Devon stood up and came to lean against the railing next to him. "Sigh one more time, and I'm siccing Kelsey on you."

Bas shook his head. "I'm fine," he said. "Thanks again for letting us tag along tonight."

Devon bumped his shoulder. "Anytime, dude."

Ugh. Sebastian had been such an asshole.

He sighed. Again.

And just that quickly Devon pulled out his phone and threateningly opened up FaceTime.

Bas threw up his hands. "I relent. I swear, no more sighing."

"Good." Devon pocketed his cell. "So why don't you just tell me what's going on?"

"I—" Bas stifled another sigh just in time. "I guess I spent my whole life feeling like an outsider in our family, but only just recently realized that all of that distance was of my own making."

Silence, then Devon rubbed his hand over his face. "Look,"

he said. "I was in your boat before. I didn't make an effort—" Bas opened his mouth, but Devon cut him off. "Sorry. Effort isn't the right word. I just mean I was really good at keeping people at a distance. I mean, hockey was a great excuse. Gone half the year, training for most of my off time. Then starting a new business."

"Yeah," Bas agreed.

"But I also realized that I spent a good part of my life being lonely."

Bas's gaze flashed to Devon's. "What?"

"I know." His brother grinned like the goofball he was. "With all my adoring fans, it's hard to imagine that *I* could be lonely."

Sebastian rolled his eyes. "So, what did you do?"

A shrug. "I met Becca. She was alone, and I guess just being with her made me realize how lucky I was. I only had one sister, one mom, one dad, one . . ." He sighed. "Something else."

"Brother, you idiot," Bas said, but he was smiling.

"Oh yeah, one of those." Devon's expression went serious. "I'm glad you're here tonight, dude. I felt like I kept reaching out to you and . . ."

Bas winced. "Stonewalled?" Devon nodded. "Shit. I'm sorry. I know it's not important now, but I guess as a kid I always felt like dad went to your stuff and mom to Kelsey's and I was just lost in the shuffle a lot of the time."

"I could see that," Devon said, surprising him. "Hockey was every weekend and multiple weeknights for year after year. I lived at the rink. And Kelsey, well at least, hockey had a season. Her engineering stuff never stopped."

"It's ridiculous to be upset about this as an adult," Bas argued. "Mom and dad did the best they could. I shouldn't—"

Devon cut him off by plunking a hand on his shoulder. "So, this may be a newsflash for you, bro, but you are allowed to have feelings." A squeeze. "Some even say they make you human."

"Being human sucks, sometimes," Bas grumbled.

"Seriously. And don't forget getter older," Devon said. "Hell, I'm getting pudgy around the middle just looking at those ravioli."

The ravioli in question had been demolished so quickly by the three of them that they'd ordered another plate to arrive when Rachel showed up. But also, pudgy was a relative term, considering the fact that Devon was in as good of shape now as he'd been when he was playing.

"You've got a fucking six-pack."

Devon dipped his finger into the sauce remaining on the plate and brought it to his mouth. "Used to be an eight-pack."

If Devon weren't his brother, Bas might be tempted to hate him.

There was a knock at the door and Pascal, Devon's body-guard, poked his head in. "A Rachel Morris has arrived—"

Becca shoved past him, Rachel in tow. "Look who I found lurking around."

"Hey, Dev," Bas said as they walked over to their women. "Can you do me a favor?"

Devon glanced down at him. "Anything."

One word, but Bas knew he meant it.

"Don't stop reaching out, okay?" He shrugged then recalled a joke they'd had from way back, when Devon had first been figuring out how to curse.

Because all professional athletes *needed* to know how to curse.

The trouble was that Devon's curse word knowledge had been limited to a single word.

"I'll attempt to get my fucking head out of my fucking ass," he said.

Devon hooted as they reached Rachel and Becca. "I'd totally forgotten about that."

"Just doing my part," Bas replied and chuckled when Devon punched him on the shoulder.

"You doing your part was the problem, if I remember." A grin. "Babe," he said and laced his arms with Becca's. "I've got to tell you this story. I think Sebastian must have been six when I got it in my head that I needed to learn how to use *all* the curse words . . ."

Bas wasn't sure how his brother finished the story—or *rather* how much he exaggerated Bas's expansion of Devon's curse word repertoire. He'd added the fucking part to round out Devon's head and ass statement, something that had made his family laugh hysterically for years after the event.

He mentally shrugged. He'd always been an observer and as such, had learned many a useful thing.

"Hi," he said.

Except for suave greetings, apparently.

But Rachel didn't seem to mind. Instead, she reached up and wrapped her arms around his neck, hugging him tightly. "I missed you."

"I'm so glad you're here." He mock-glared. "Finally."

Her cheeks went slightly rosy. "It's been a crazy week, but I made it in the end."

Fingers brushed along her jaw. "Thanks for coming, sweetheart."

"Are you kidding?" She gestured to the space around them. "Look at this. It's incredible, and you've totally spoiled me for the cheap seats now."

"Me, too," he said. "I never knew it could be like this."

"Well you both do now," Devon said, coming over and herding them so they could see the ice. The third period would be starting in just a few minutes. "And Rachel, once you succumb to the power of the ravioli, you'll never watch a Gold game any other way."

"Ravioli?" Rachel asked.

"It's *ah*-mazing good," Becca said then winked conspiratorially. "We ate the first plate, but another should be up soon."

"I'm starving." Rachel lifted her elbows to the sides, as if pretending to get ready to tackle someone. "Am I going to have to fight the pregnant lady for it?" The playfulness in her tone, the giggles, and subsequent fake-trash talk she exchanged with Becca just cemented to Bas that his woman was the stuff of legend.

Fuck, but I love you, he thought.

It wasn't until the three other people in the suite whirled to face him that Sebastian realized he'd spoken aloud.

"Uhh," Becca said, taking one look at Rachel's pale face and what was probably a horrified expression on his face. "I—*we* need to go get . . . something." Then she grabbed Devon's arm and all but dragged him from the box.

He barely heard them leave, his focus was so fixed on Rachel.

She was breathing . . . rapidly and too shallow.

"I'm sorry," he blurted. "I didn't—"

She lifted a hand, half curled in on herself. But though her words were interspersed with gasping breaths, her words were fierce. "Don't," she said. "Don't . . . you . . . fucking take . . . it back."

Bas knelt in front of her. "I couldn't take it back," he said, going for gentle though his pulse was pounding and cold sweat dripped down his spine. What if she didn't feel the same? What if she wanted to end things before they really got going? What if this was too much too soon and she ran? "I couldn't take it back, sweetheart, because I love you so fucking deeply that I'd have to tear out my own heart and stomp on it to have any hope to stop loving you."

Tears leaked out of the corners of her eyes, and he hurried to wipe them away. "Even then I think I'd still love you because you're not just in here—" He brought her hand to his chest, above his racing heart. "You're in my brain, my body, my soul. And I'm sorry I blurted it out like that, but I swear I fell half in love with you the first moment I met you."

Finally, she seemed to unfreeze. Her eyes locked on his and her mouth curved. "Only half?" she asked.

Bas's lungs suddenly began working again. "The other half was reserved for you tipping over that bowl of salad dressing."

"You made me waste an entire bottle of Ranch," she groaned. Her smile grew as she tugged him to his feet and hugged him. "I'm sorry I panicked," she whispered as he held her tightly for one long quiet moment.

He pulled back, nose wrinkling. "I'm sorry I announced it in front of my brother and his wife and didn't save it for a romantic, candlelit dinner or something."

Rachel opened her mouth, but her words were interrupted by a knock.

Becca poked her head in. "Sorry to interrupt, but"—she revealed a large plate full of ravioli with a flourish—"*ravioli* are here!"

Rachel pressed a kiss to his lips. "I'd take a thousand real moments with you over one fancy candlelit dinner."

Devon sent him a questioning look, mouthed, "Is it okay?"

Bas nodded and his heart was full as they all gathered around the table at the front of the box and sat down to stuff their mouths.

Oh, and to watch the Gold trounce their opponents, there was that, too.

"For the record," Rachel whispered after they'd demolished the pasta and chatted and thoroughly joked around. "First, your brother and Becca are amazing."

He touched her cheek, kissed the tip of her nose. "And the second?"

She spoke to the group. "That ravioli is the shit."

They all cracked up and Bas couldn't help feeling that this was one of the best nights of his life.

Especially when Rachel reached laughing lips up to his ear to murmur, "Number three is that . . . I love you, too."

Yup.

Best night ever.

TWENTY-ONE

Rachel

RACHEL AND SEBASTIAN said goodnight to Devon and Becca then caught an Uber to Bas's apartment, since it was closer.

She waited until they were through the door and the panel locked behind them before she announced, "I have something to tell you."

He froze, a slice of doubt crossing his face.

Damn. She'd meant it as a playful tease, not to make him feel insecure.

"Did I—"

Acting quickly before he could hop completely aboard the unsure train, Rachel reached for the hem of her Gold jersey and yanked it up and over her head.

"Rach—?"

Her long-sleeved tee followed, leaving her in only her bra.

The very sexy amethyst bra Sebastian had bought her.

She flicked open the button on her jeans, undid the zipper,

and pushed them down, stepping out of them and her shoes at the same time.

He made a noise that sounded as if he'd swallowed his tongue.

Rachel slowly turned in a circle. "*This* is what I wanted to tell you," she said. "Or rather, *show* you."

His face was a study of lines—two brows slashing down and together, a pair of lips pressed flat, a jaw clenched tightly—and she would have almost said that he was angry if not for the heat in his eyes.

Storm-ravaged eyes slid down her body. Back up. Heat prickled everywhere that gaze traveled and . . . since it traveled pretty much everywhere, she suddenly felt as though she had been dropped inside a boiling pot and was roasting from the inside out.

She took a step toward him, but he extended a hand, one palm out.

"Turn around again?"

It was a rasping plea and one she couldn't have resisted obeying even if she'd tried.

Slowly, she spun in one more circle.

Bas's hands were clenched tightly into fists when she faced him again. "I don't care how much it will cost me, but you're never wearing anything else."

She laughed. "A G-string might not go over too well in the office."

"I disagree." A smirk. "I know I would be a hell of a lot more productive if I knew you were waiting for me."

"I *am* waiting for you," she challenged.

"There's waiting," he said. "And there's anticipation."

"I've anticipated this for weeks now," she murmured then reached up and unhooked her bra. It landed almost soundlessly on the floor.

His eyes went somehow hotter.

"How's that for anticipation?"

A slow, heated smile before he curled a finger in her direction. "Come here."

She took a step back. "No. I think I should torture you like you've been torturing me. Let's take it slow, Rachel," she mimicked. "We have all the time in the world and meanwhile, I'm dripping wet and—*oof!*"

Bas swept her up into his arms. His lips collided with hers, his tongue slipping into her mouth, tangling with hers. Approximately two heartbeats or maybe two minutes or hell, she didn't know, the man kissed her so senseless that it could have been two hours before her back was pressed against his mattress.

"Now what was that about wet?" he asked, fingers sliding under the waistband of her underwear and between her thighs.

She moaned when he brushed her clit, hardly noticed when he tugged her underwear down her legs and off. But she certainly did notice when he bent and gave her the hottest kiss of her life.

And not on her mouth.

His tongue flicked over her, settling into a rhythm that quickly had her writhing and begging for . . . what? More? Yes. But the finger he slipped inside wasn't enough.

She wanted Bas, hot and hard and *deep* inside her.

"Please," she gasped then groaned when he did something with his tongue that made her toes curl and slid another finger inside. Suddenly, she wasn't thinking about the empty, aching feeling, but rather, was concentrating on the pleasure spiraling from her center and moving outward, tightening all her muscles, tilting her head back toward the ceiling.

Sweat beaded on her skin, heat coiling in her scalp, her breasts, her—

He nipped her, a little rough but she'd needed rough,

needed something intense enough to burst through the sensations engulfing her, needed something to focus all that pleasure to a single pinprick so that it . . . would . . .

Explode.

"Fuck!" she cried and bucked hard. Bas held her in place, licking and kissing her through the peak and down the other side.

And then she just lay there, chest heaving, limbs completely limp.

It wasn't just from the pleasure either. Because, yes, that was fan-fucking-tastic, but Rachel somehow felt both completely shattered and totally intact. Almost as though Bas had taken her apart piece by piece and then carefully glued her back together again.

But she wasn't Humpty Dumpty, damaged and more fragile than before.

Bas had made her stronger.

She didn't even realize that she'd started crying until he crawled up next to her and tugged her into his arms. Rachel burrowed herself into his chest.

"I'm sorry," she said. "It's not you." A sniff. "Well, I guess it *is* you—"

He pressed a kiss to her forehead. "Since you came apart on my tongue, I'm going to assume that those were screams of pleasure, not pain."

She snorted. "Considering I was using your hair as handles to grind myself against your mouth, I'd say that was a safe bet." Her eyes slid closed, but not before she saw him smile. "I love you, Bas," she said softly. "And I guess just feeling that, knowing that you're in it with me, makes everything so much better."

Fingers on her nape, her cheekbone, her jaw. "I like that everything is better."

"Me, too. But"—her hand slid down—"I think I can save the

talking for later, don't you think? I have a *little* problem to take care of."

He groaned and thrusted into her hand as she gripped him. "Fuck, baby." A beat. "I think, normally, I'd be insulted by the term *little*, but if you're going to stroke me like that, you can call me whatever you want."

Rachel followed the path of her hand, loving the way he jerked and cursed as she took his cock in her mouth.

"Sweetheart."

"Mmm." Her tongue traced the underside of his erection.

He hissed. "Baby."

She sucked him deep into the back of her throat and matched the strokes of her tongue to those of her hand.

For all of five seconds.

"Oof!" she said again, but before another outrage noise could escape her, or hell, before she could crawl back down Sebastian's body and continue sucking him like her favorite lollipop, he'd reached over her to grab a condom from the nightstand and rolled it on.

"Please say you're with me," he gritted out.

Her only answer was to wrap her legs around his waist and tug him down.

He pushed home, and, *fuck*, but that was the absolute best feeling in the world.

"You good?" he asked.

"Stop worrying," she said. "Just love me, Bas. Love me with everything you have."

He bent, brushed his lips to hers. "Always, sweetheart."

And then he moved, stroking in and out, bringing them both higher and higher until they crashed over the peak and tumbled into orgasm.

They were lying together afterward, limbs tangled, sweat

dampening their skin, breaths in rapid gasps, when he rotated his head to face her.

Lips curved he said, "I am man, hear me roar. I'm so glad I've found the right part-*ner*."

She burst into laughter.

Somehow, she'd just been fucked into near oblivion, was lying in bed with the man who brought her there, and she was laughing.

Laughing.

"God, I love you," she said and kissed him, a long, slow, joyful kiss that filled her cells with champagne—bubbling, hopeful, and effervescent.

Perfect. Bas was absolutely, imperfectly, perfect for her.

TWENTY-TWO

Sebastian

MONDAY.

And it had been a Monday.

Clay and Heather were back from their working honeymoon, which meant that employees at Steele Technologies, and presumably RoboTech as well, were running around like crazy, readying and attempting to implement all of the ideas the bosses had brainstormed on their trip.

Rachel had texted him earlier in the day saying that she was banning Heather from any form of vacation for the foreseeable future.

No more time off. Nope. No way. No how.

He sent back:

Bad over there?

The worst. Heather has BIG ideas.

Bas had grinned.

They're probably really good big ideas.

Yes. Yes, they are. Which makes this even worse.

Considering that Clay had been on a similar warpath that morning, Bas could sympathize. He also knew how to make things better for Rachel.

Tonight. My place. Documentary on WWII, takeout, and pajamas.

Throw in a glass of wine and I'm in.

He'd agreed, of course, having already stocked his cupboards with Rachel's preferred brand. This was the woman he loved, and he wanted her to have everything she could possibly want.

Thankfully, he had that evening to look forward to when Clay strolled into his office mid-morning and dropped another project on his lap.

It was the type of project Bas had been dying to sink his teeth into.

But also one he didn't think he could do properly. Not with everything else already on his plate.

"Before you give me that look," his boss said. "Check the file underneath."

Bas flipped open the folder. "Uhh." He stared at the stack of papers, started flipping through one resume after another. "Either you're trying to fire me"—his gaze flashed up—"or . . ."

Clay's mouth quirked. "It's the *or*," he said. "I'd like you to hire your replacement so you can take on a new job title. You'll find the proposal for that in the file below." He sat in the chair in front of Bas's desk, leaned back, and crossed his legs at his ankles. "You're wasted as my assistant, have been for a long time, and I'll admit that I'm not looking forward to losing you in that role. You've been the best I've ever had."

"I—" Bas shook his head as he stared at the proposal. VP of Acquisitions. "I'm not sure I have the qualifications for—"

"Sebastian," Clay said, putting up a palm. "You've been streamlining the projects Steele pursues for months now. Think of it this way, I want to take the rest of the job—flights, schedule, email filtering—off your hands so you can focus on that."

Put it that way.

"You sure that—?"

Clay narrowed his eyes. "My future VP of Acquisitions wouldn't finish that question."

Noted.

Bas nodded.

"Good," Clay said and stood. "These are the rejects from when I hired you. One of them might be able to live up to your standards, or we might have to start from scratch." He turned for the door. "I'll trust your judgment on that."

Bas rose to his feet. "I'll narrow it down to a couple of candidates then bring you in on the final decision."

Clay paused on the threshold. "And that right there."

Bas frowned, waited for his boss to finish the sentence. When he didn't, Bas asked, "What's right there?"

"Why you won't just stop at VP."

With that, Clay left Bas standing there, mouth gaped open like a fish.

He slumped down into his chair, heart pounding, excitement racing through every nerve. Holy shit, this was actually going to happen. Picking up his cell, he texted Rachel.

I have something awesome to tell you.

When she didn't reply back within a few minutes, as was typical, he settled down to work his way through the stack of résumés. She was probably in a meeting or bogged down with Heather's grand ideas.

So, he pushed his cell to the side and got started on Clay's grand idea.

"Hey."

The female voice startled him, and he glanced up from the papers to see Kelsey standing at his office door.

His eyes flicked to his phone, saw that several hours had passed and that it was nearly lunchtime. A blip of unease settled in his stomach when he saw that Rachel still hadn't texted back.

But then Kelsey was striding into the room. "Come on, little bro," she snapped. "At least act like you're happy to see me."

Bas stood and crossed the room, phone in hand. "I *am* happy to see you," he said. "Sorry, it's just that Rachel . . ."

When he trailed off, she asked. "Rachel, what? Oh, no. Don't tell me you two broke up. I really like her and would hate to disown you." She grinned. "Because I would definitely choose her over you."

In the past, those words would have probably hurt him.

Today, he took them as intended: as a joke and nothing more.

"Hilarious," he deadpanned. His stomach churned, unable to shake the feeling that something wasn't quite right. Rachel had never gone this long without at least sending him a quick text saying she'd be out of touch.

Kelsey took one look at his face. "It was a joke," she said. "You know that, right?"

Bas pulled her into a hug. "Reading that loud and clear." He frowned. "I just—hang on a second, okay?"

He sent Rachel another text.

Sweetheart, all good?

No reply.

He shook it off. Rachel was probably in a meeting.

"Sorry," he told Kelsey. "It's silly, but I haven't heard from Rachel all morning and—"

"What?" she asked softly. "You're not exactly the clingy type, Sebastian, so I'm guessing there's another part to this story?"

"Her ex-husband is a . . ."

"Tool?" Kelsey supplied.

"Times that by about a million," he said, not wanting to reveal what the sick son-of-a-bitch had done to Rachel. That was her business. But he also wasn't about to minimize what Preston had done. "He—" Bas shook his head. "It's much better for her to not be with him."

Kelsey, apparently, read between the lines. "Is he dangerous?"

"To Rachel? Yes," he said. "But last we heard, he was still living in Iowa and she has a restraining order."

"Hm." Kelsey frowned. "Those don't always work, you know."

Bas glared at her.

"I'm just saying."

"Yeah." He sighed. "I'll give her a little more time. Her boss just got back from a business trip, so she's probably bogged down."

Kelsey nodded. "You're probably right," she agreed. "I didn't mean to bug you at work," she said as he stared at his phone screen. "But I was in town for a conference and wanted to see if you were available to grab lunch."

His eyes shot to hers, surprised. "I'd like that," he said.

Except the decision to give Rachel more time wasn't sitting well in his gut.

"But do you think we can swing by Rachel's office on the way out? It's not far."

Kelsey clapped him on the shoulder. "You know what, little bro?"

He walked over to his desk and grabbed his wallet from the drawer, sticking it along with his phone into his pockets. "What?"

"You're a good guy."

He snorted. "So effusive with the praise." But he hugged her. "Seriously, though, thanks for stopping by. I've wanted to—"

"See me?" she interrupted and fluttered her hands in front of her face. "Oh, you're so sweet, Sebastian. Just the best brother in the world."

"Dork," he said, but relief poured through him that she hadn't argued about the pit stop. He just needed to lay eyes on Rachel, reassure him that the anxiousness in his gut was an over-reaction. He was probably just on edge because they'd spent so much time together over the weekend that he was in Rachel-withdrawal or some shit.

He tugged Kelsey's ponytail. "What I *was* going to say is that I've been wanting to find out how the new job was going."

Her face softened, and he was doubly glad he'd asked. Yes, he'd already decided to put the past aside, forget the resentment, and focus on rebuilding his bonds with his family, and Kelsey's visit proved that she wanted to strengthen them, too. But it wasn't all about his family making up for perceived slights to him. He also needed to make things right by reaching out to them.

Look at him. All adult and shit.

She'd just finished telling him about her new boss when Clay met up with them by the elevators.

Bas introduced Kelsey.

"Sorry to interrupt your lunch," Clay said after shaking his sister's hand. "But Heather just texted me and wanted to know if you'd heard anything from Rachel. Are you guys meeting up with her to eat?"

Sebastian blinked. "No." His throat went tight. "She's at the office."

Or that's where she was supposed to be.

Clay frowned, held up his phone. "Apparently, she ran out to grab . . ."

Bas didn't hear the rest of the words. His heart had started pounding, a rapid *whoosh-whoosh* that drowned Clay out. He pulled out his cell and dialed Rachel's number. It rang four times before going to voice mail.

Fuck. He called again.

Same thing.

Fingers shaking, he typed out a text.

Rachel. Are you okay? Heather hasn't heard from you and neither have I. We're both worried.

He held his breath as he waited for one eternal minute.

Nothing.

He turned to Kelsey. "I'm sorry—"

"Go," she said then called, "Wait!" when he took off for the stairs. "What's her address?"

Bas rattled it off and ran.

TWENTY-THREE

Rachel

RACHEL HOPPED out of the Uber and raced through the front door of her apartment building. She had maybe fifteen minutes to grab the file she'd forgotten that morning and to stuff some much-needed sustenance in her face.

It was bizarre that she'd had to run home in the middle of the day.

She always double and triple-checked her bag, making sure she had everything she could possibly need.

And everything she *couldn't* possibly need.

But today she'd forgotten the file that Heather needed for a meeting that afternoon and, idiot of all idiots, *she* had taken it home just to make sure it was perfect.

Another reason to go solely digital, she thought, hurrying over to the elevator and jabbing the button. Of course, Trace McPearson didn't trust technology and had resisted even getting involved with RoboTech at all.

As a bone, she and Heather provided old-school Trace with actual paper files.

Which apparently, she'd left at home because her brain was rotting.

Less than a month after falling in love with a man who was sweet and sexy and so good in bed and she spent half her time dreaming about jumping Sebastian and the other half thinking about all the ways she could squeeze more time out of her schedule to see him more.

Because almost every night and weekend wasn't enough.

She wanted it all.

Smiling at that thought, because a year ago she never would have expected that a man could quickly become her best friend, Rachel stepped off the elevator and hurried over to her door.

She input the code on the keypad, waiting for the metal against metal sound of the lock disengaging then pushed inside.

And her heart stopped, bile burned the back of her throat, her knees went weak.

Then she remembered all of the self-defense classes she had gone to. She remembered her instructor's voice yelling at her, drilling it into that that she should always take the opportunity to run.

So she moved.

Whirling around, she scrambled for the door handle.

Too late.

White-hot agony ripped through her scalp as Preston grabbed a chunk of her hair and wrenched her head back.

"Did you honestly think I would let you get away with it?" he hissed.

"Preston—"

He shook her roughly and she cried out in pain. "I didn't say you could speak." He slammed her head forward and into the door. Something cracked—her nose?—and blood began gushing down her face. Then he punched her hard in the side and something else cracked.

This time, she knew exactly what had broken. Her ribs.

"You're so stupid." He breathed in her face, hot, rotten breath that made her stomach churn. "You came home for this, didn't you?" A hard *smack* of a file against her cheek. "You're so predictable. I knew, just knew, you'd come back for it."

She shook her head and received another slam of her face against the door. "Yes," he said. "I know you, darling. Know how unobservant you are. Know your patterns." He twisted the hand in her hair, forcing her eyes to his. "You used your fucking birthday as the code to your apartment, you dumb bitch."

Her eyes filled with tears. It had been idiotic to use that date.

"You didn't even notice I'd been in here, did you?"

Rachel couldn't catch her breath.

Preston didn't care. He shook her. "*Did* you?"

"N-no," she whispered.

"I even left you a clue. I never would have stood by and allowed a mess like this fucking pigsty in my house." He whipped her around. "Shoes everywhere, coats not hung up, wine bottles in the fridge. You're a slob. And a whore."

"No."

Another slam of her body against the door. This time it was her back, and the movement knocked the wind out of her all over again.

"A whore," he repeated. "Fucking another man when you used to spread your legs for me."

Just words, she reminded herself. They were just words, sharpened and aimed to defeat her before she could mount a fight, to hurt her so deeply that she'd just lie down and die.

Not today.

Preston still had a tight grip on her hair.

But her hands were free.

They were slippery, but she focused all her effort on

reaching slowly behind her for the knob, not on the hate her ex-husband was spewing, nor on the pain that had black creeping rapidly into the edges of her vision.

If she passed out now, he'd kill her.

If she didn't get out of the apartment, he'd kill her.

She knew both of those things instinctively.

So, the moment she felt the knob turn, she shifted and let her bag—which had somehow stayed on her shoulder—slide down to her wrist. Lurching forward, Rachel brought it up toward Preston's head at the same time she yanked the door open.

Preston cursed as the leather collided with his face.

It didn't knock him out, the bag wasn't heavy enough for that, but it did startle him enough that he cursed and let go of her hair.

She slipped out of the door and sprinted down the hallway, screaming for help.

Then made it all of ten steps before Preston was on her again.

"Shut up," he said and punched her in the stomach, before dragging her back toward her apartment.

"No!" she gasped and sucked in a painful breath before yelling at the top of her lungs, "Help! *Someone help me!*" She clawed at his arms, punching and kicking and biting anything she could reach.

But he was stronger.

No matter how hard she fought, he just kept pulling her down the hall. She kicked at the walls, grabbed onto the narrow indentation of a doorframe and continued screaming.

Anything. *Anything* to stop him.

Except it was the middle of the day. Everyone was at work.

She was alone.

Panic settled in as Preston yanked her over the threshold

and back into her apartment. Rachel hooked a foot over the frame then screamed in absolute agony as her ankle popped and gave way.

"Stupid, stupid bitch," he growled and threw her forward. She landed on her bag, the bulky leather jabbing her in the ribs.

The black that had been creeping in earlier was swirling now, grabbing at her, threatening to tug her into oblivion.

But Rachel knew she couldn't let it.

She knew she couldn't let Preston win.

Not like this. Not when she'd never fought back before. Not when she'd finally found people worth living for.

Gripping her bag tightly in one hand, she pushed herself up, staggering, teetering on one foot.

Preston had turned to lock the door, but when he rotated back to face her and saw she was standing, his mouth curved in a predatory smile.

"You finally found some spine?" he asked, his once hand-some features transforming into something cruel and dark and sick. "Did your lawyer friend convince you you'd be safe?" Cold, *cold* blue eyes locked onto hers. "I might have let you go, you know. Thank the good Lord that my useless excuse for a wife was finally gone." He took a step toward her and laughed when she scrambled back. "But that *bitch* cost my father his job. And I cannot let that stand."

Oh God. Bec.

Rachel's knees threatened to buckle. She'd brought her friend into her mess.

How could she have risked—

But then she thought about what Bec would do in this situa-tion, what Abby or CeCe or Heather or even Seraphina would do.

They wouldn't roll over and die.

They would fight.

Rachel lifted her chin.

"Do your worst, you fucking bastard." She spat at him, half blood from her gushing nose, half bile from her revulsion of the man.

He rolled his eyes. "You're a pathetic, scared little girl who is worth *nothing*."

"I'm not *her* any longer," she said, inching toward her kitchen counter. If she could just put some distance between them, buy herself some time—

He lunged.

She threw her bag again, but this time he dodged the leather satchel.

He came at her, would have actually gotten her if her leg hadn't collapsed, causing her to teeter to one side. She scrambled in that moment, Preston skidding past, her arms flailing to regain her balance and . . . landing on an empty bottle of wine.

She and Bas had finished it sometime last week and she'd left it on the counter, intending to drop it in the recycling bin on the ground floor.

But she hadn't gotten that far.

And now her fingers slid around the neck of the bottle and she gripped it tightly.

Preston turned, face drawn into a feral expression.

Rachel didn't think, just lifted the bottle and with every last bit of strength she possessed, brought it down onto his head.

It shattered into a thousand pieces, pain shot through her palm, up her arm . . . and Preston?

His lunge didn't halt.

He took her to the ground, landing squarely on top of her.

The agony of her ankle, her nose, her ribs, and hand . . . it was too much.

The black sucked her under.

TWENTY-FOUR

Sebastian

HE RACED into the lobby and was immediately stopped by a police officer.

"I need—" he broke off, trying to push around him. "My girlfriend—"

"This is a crime scene," the officer said. "You'll need to wait here."

Bas shook his head. He couldn't wait there. He needed to get to Rachel. "No," he snapped. "Where is she?" He shoved the officer hard. "Let me go, you fucking—"

"Cortez," a slightly accented voice Bas didn't immediately recognize said. "He's with me."

The officer nodded and with an exceptionally dirty look, let Sebastian slip under the caution tape.

A hand stopped his headlong rush for the stairs.

Bas finally turned and studied the owner of the voice. Pascal, his brother's bodyguard. In a heartbeat, he remembered Kelsey asking for Rachel's address. She must have called Devon, who'd sent Pascal. The bodyguard had connections in the police department, and the promise of more information finally had Bas's brain clearing.

"Wait," Pascal said. "Let me find out where she is."

He nodded, and Pascal went over to speak with another officer.

But it turned out that he didn't need Pascal to find out where Rachel was because at that moment, the elevator doors opened with a ding and a stretcher was rolled out.

The woman he loved was black and blue and on a stretcher.

Bas didn't think, he just ran.

Rachel was unconscious, her face covered in blood, bruises already mottling the surface, her leg was twisted in an odd direction and . . .

His woman was broken and bleeding and—

Fuck.

Sebastian's eyes stung.

Pascal grabbed his arm, tugging him after the stretcher when his feet had frozen in horror. "It's superficial," he said and pushed Bas toward the waiting ambulance. "Go with her. I'll get your family to the hospital."

Bas nodded.

The paramedics didn't complain when he jumped into the back of the ambulance. He watched as they worked on Rachel, relaxing slightly when they weren't rushing and didn't seem overly concerned.

"Three minutes to the hospital," the paramedic told Bas.

He managed another nod but couldn't take his eyes off Rachel, couldn't help but burn every single bruise and mark into his brain. The bastard was going to pay.

"I've never seen a scene like that," the paramedic said into the silence. She was a middle-aged woman, blond hair laced heavily with gray.

Bas bristled at the awe in her tone.

What the fuck was wrong with her? His woman was hurt, and she was coveting the violence?

"I've never seen someone fight so hard to stay alive." Gentle brown eyes met his. "She must have really wanted to see you again."

His anger faded, replaced with so much love that he knew if Rachel didn't wake up something inside of him would be permanently broken.

The ambulance slowed to a halt, and she reached across to squeeze his arm.

"She's going to be okay here"—the paramedic indicated Rachel's body—"but she's going to need some help here and here"—she pointed at Rachel's heart and head—"Don't let her go it alone, okay?"

"I won't."

The back doors opened and they wheeled Rachel into the Emergency Department.

SEVERAL HOURS LATER, Bas was still in the waiting room. He'd tried to follow the stretcher into the actual department, wanting Rachel to see a familiar and safe face the moment she woke, but the nurses had stopped him, redirecting him to an empty chair outside the reception desk.

He hadn't been alone long, Devon arriving within a half hour, followed by Becca and Kelsey.

His parents had called, wanting to fly out, but Bas had told them to wait.

He'd texted Clay and pretty soon, the waiting room was filled with Heather, CeCe, Sera, and Bec and their spouses. The only ones who were missing were Jordan, who was on a business trip, and Abby, who was scrambling to find a sitter so she could come down.

And still they hadn't heard a word about how Rachel was doing.

The calm assurance from the paramedic who'd wheeled her into the back had long since vanished, and Sebastian was probably only minutes from storming through the doors and risking arrest.

Because there was a new addition to the waiting room.

A pair of police officers standing, arms crossed, in front of the door that led to the actual ER.

Bec was pacing back and forth on the floor, talking softly into her cell, trying to find out exactly what had happened and not getting much of anywhere.

Rachel was back there and she was alone and—

The doors to the back opened, and a nurse came out. "Sebastian Scott?"

He was on his feet and moving before she even finished saying his name.

"I'm Sebastian," he said.

"Come with me." She led him down an anemic looking hallway and into a room.

Rachel was inside.

She had a large bandage on her forehead, several smaller ones on her nose and cheeks. Her top lip was swollen, both eyes blackened. One arm was wrapped in gauze and cradled close to her chest and her right leg was encased in a cast from foot to knee.

He'd wanted to kill the bastard before, now Sebastian wanted to absolutely eviscerate Preston Johnston.

"Hi," she rasped.

Bas rushed over to her bedside, but once there, he extended one arm and froze, not sure where he could touch her.

She lifted her uninjured hand and cupped his cheek. "Hey, you."

There were tears in his eyes. He knew it and didn't give a damn. "I'm so sorry," he said. "I should have—" he began, even knowing there was nothing anyone could have done. That they couldn't have anticipated Preston would have come after her then, couldn't have known he'd be in her apartment waiting for her. He'd gone eighteen months without a peep, and Bas had expected the bastard would fade into oblivion.

The nurse glanced over at the police officers, who'd come to stand by either side of the door to Rachel's room. They nodded.

"You should both know that the . . . other patient"—a hint of venom in her tone—"didn't make it."

"What?" Rachel said.

"The male who arrived with you didn't survive," she said. "I thought you might sleep better tonight knowing that." A beat as she glanced at Sebastian. "That *both* of you might sleep better."

"I didn't—" Rachel shook her head.

Fingers rested on her shoulder. "He had a bleed. One that had been leaking slowly for a long time. It could have gone at any time." A reassuring squeeze. "Today just happened to be that day."

"But I hit him with the bottle so hard."

The nurse straightened, indicating Rachel's bound hand. "I think you injured yourself more than him with that bottle shattering the way it did. The coroner said he was likely gone before it even made contact."

"I—"

One of the officers handed him a card and murmured they'd need a statement at some point the next day. Bas told her they'd be in touch, and the officers left Rachel's room.

"It's over," the nurse said when they'd gone. "Just hold on to that thought for now. The rest can come later."

Rachel nodded and her eyes were misty when they met Sebastian's. "It's really over?"

He nodded. "Yes."

"Can I go home now?"

"What?" Bas said. "No. You need to stay and—"

"Actually," the nurse said. "All of her scans are clear and while she's bruised to hell and back, Rachel is very lucky. Aside from broken bones, she doesn't have any serious injuries."

"*Bones?*" he ground out.

"Just some tiny ones," Rachel said.

The nurse rolled her eyes, but she was smiling. "Several of the small bones in her foot are broken. The orthopedist has set her leg already, but she'll need several follow up appointments with her as well as an internist, just to confirm her broken ribs are healing properly."

Bas stiffened. "Why in the hell is she coming home if she has that many injuries?"

"Because she's going to be okay and doesn't need observation. Which means the best thing for her right now is to recover at home." The nurse began typing on the computer in the room. "I'll grab her discharge instructions and then go over them with you both."

Rachel glanced at him. "So my apartment is . . ."

A crime scene, probably. A horrible reminder of what had happened, definitely.

"Want to borrow mine?" he asked.

And the smile she gave him went a long way to soothing the anger and panic and absolute fury that was engulfing his heart.

A NURSE WHEELED Rachel out of the back and then, when she pointed, in the direction of their group.

"Fuck," Devon hissed as they came close. "That son of a bitch is going to die a slow death."

"Dev," Bas warned.

His brother ignored him, moving to kneel next to Rachel. "I'm having my car brought around. Do you know where you want to stay tonight? I can get you a hotel or you can stay with—"

"Bas?" she asked softly.

"The bed hog is staying with me," he replied.

Her lips tipped up into a small smile.

She would be okay. They would both be okay.

"You're getting a raise," Heather bawled.

Rachel frowned then winced. "What are you talking about?"

"I don't know," Heather said with a sniff as Clay tugged her into his arms. She buried her face into his chest, shoulders shaking.

Sera pressed a kiss to an unbruised part of her face. "I'm just so glad you're okay."

CeCe hugged her with extreme gentleness. "Abby wanted me to tell you that she'll make sure you get the good drugs."

Rachel snorted, then brought her hand to her middle. "Don't make me laugh, it hurts too much."

Bec had been standing in the background, but at those words, she finally knelt in front of Rachel, her eyes were wet, her nose red and dripping. "I'm so sorry. I should have—"

"Shut. Up." Rachel's harsh tone took them all by surprise. "There is not one person in this room who has any right to feel guilty"—her gaze flicked from Bec to Sebastian—"*Not* one person. Okay?"

Bec sniffed, started to shake her head—

"Bec," Rachel snapped. "Not. One. Person."

Bec shuddered but eventually nodded.

Pascal poked his head in, indicating the car was ready, and they all made their way to it, helping the nurse get Rachel settled into the back of Devon's sedan.

A few minutes later, her friends had all said goodbye and made promises to check up on Rachel tomorrow, and Kelsey was herding Becca and Devon into her rental car.

"Call me later," Devon said.

"I'd better be on that call list, too," Kelsey called before closing the driver's side door.

Somehow, despite everything, Sebastian smiled.

Eventually they would all be okay.

He'd make damn sure of that.

TWENTY-FIVE

Rachel

A WEEK LATER, Rachel finally forced Bas to go back to work.

Bas's overprotection had become both endearing and infuriating. He'd even carried her to the bathroom that morning before he'd left for the office, for fuck's sake. Her leg was broken and, *okay* so were two of her ribs, but she had one of those knee scooter things and could totally make it to the toilet.

Then there was the fact that he'd been watching her every waking moment, as though he expected her to crack.

Fine, she'd half-expected to lose it herself.

The terror of that day, of the minutes that felt like hours, an eternity, still flashed across her mind at all moments.

But . . . she'd been through it before.

She knew she'd get through it again.

And this time, she had people who loved her by her side.

That didn't mean she wasn't going more than a little stir-crazy. She was used to being busy, used to working or thinking about work during most waking hours.

It had been T-minus seven days since she'd checked her email, and her inbox was going to be the absolute worst.

Plus, she'd already watched what felt like every documentary on Netflix.

Sleep hadn't been coming all that easily, and lying in the dark was much less desirable than staying up all hours bingeing on her history and political docs.

It wasn't every time she closed her eyes, and it was definitely happening less frequently as the days went on, but Rachel could still feel the bottle colliding with Preston's head, could remember the absolute terror, the burning pain filling her body.

The police had come, and she'd given her statement. They'd confirmed that he'd had an aneurysm and had been dead before he'd fallen on top of her. They'd also revealed that she hadn't actually been alone that morning.

Three apartments down, a teenager had been home sick from school. She'd called 9-1-1 and they'd shown up seconds after Rachel had passed out.

After Preston had died.

Fuck.

Why did she feel guilty?

Because deep down, Rachel was relieved he was gone, that he wouldn't be coming back to hurt her all over again.

Did that make her a bad person?

Maybe. Maybe not.

Or maybe it just made her normal?

She'd sent the girl a thank you note but knew that she needed to meet her, make sure she wasn't terrorized by what she'd heard, what she'd seen.

The last thing Rachel wanted was for anyone else to be hurt because of Preston.

Sighing, she shifted carefully in bed, her cracked ribs still not happy with any sort of movement. Heather had forbidden Rachel from doing any sort of work, but Abby had understood that Rachel had needed a distraction, and so she'd stolen a laptop from RoboTech and smuggled it into Bas's apartment with all the pomp and secrecy of a secret agent.

Smiling and shaking her head, Rachel knew she'd been so lucky to have found such a great group of people.

They'd had a virtual parade of visitors through the apartment, Abby and Jordan bringing the stolen laptop along with enough snacks to fill the cabinets to bursting. Sera had come bearing a new set of pajamas that buttoned on top and with legs wide enough to easily slip over her cast. CeCe and Colin had brought dinner then stayed to keep them company for several hours. CeCe had even gone so far as to book all of Rachel's follow-up appointments and then had run out to pick up the refills for her prescriptions. Even Devon, Becca, and Kelsey had come by with Bas's parents in tow, and his mom had made the most incredible spaghetti for all of them.

But as Rachel booted up the laptop and started making her way through her emails, there was one person who hadn't come.

And that was the real problem keeping her up at night.

How could she make Bec understand that what had happened with Preston wasn't her fault?

Well, she certainly couldn't do anything with one bum leg and aching ribs. Except . . . she smiled. Maybe she *could* do something.

She picked up her cell and sent a text.

I'm alone and need food. Can you bring Molly's?

Almost instantly, Bec texted her back.

I'll be there in thirty.

And so, another one fell into her trap. Rachel snorted at her own joke then got down to emails for another twenty minutes before carefully sliding out of bed. It'd take her close to ten minutes just to get to the door.

An exaggeration, yes, but only a slight one.

But it was a good thing she'd gotten up when she had because the knock came when she was still a few feet from the door. Her phone buzzed.

It's me.

Rachel rolled forward and glanced through the peephole. If she'd taken nothing else from Preston, he'd at least taught her to be more aware of her surroundings.

Bec was on the other side of the wood, bag from Molly's in hand, a tight, pained expression pulling on her face.

Rachel opened the door. "Thank you," she said and sniffed. "You brought soup, too?"

Bec shrugged. "Seemed the thing to do."

Then she just stood there, all unsure and indecisive and totally not *Bec* at all. Normally, she'd be barging in giving orders. Today, she just stared at Rachel with regret in her eyes.

"Come in," Rachel said and wheeled herself backward.

Bec nodded, stepping over the threshold then turned to lock the door. Rachel ignored how the click of the dead bolt sliding home made her gut twist. She'd get over that.

Eventually.

"Where's Sebastian?" Bec asked.

"I got tired of him bossing me around and kicked him out." Bec's brows lifted. "To the office," Rachel added. "For eight straight hours."

Lips curving, her friend walked forward to the table and began unpacking the salads and soup. "I got you potato and leek. I thought you'd had that before, but if you don't like it, I also have butternut squash and chicken noodle." She lined up enough containers that it looked as if she'd ordered half the menu. "Oh, and tomato soup and both salads and—"

"Bec."

Her friend ignored the entreaty.

Wheels squeaking slightly as she skidded forward, Rachel closed the distance between them and placed her hand over Bec's, stilling it.

"We need to talk about it."

Bec shook her head. "That one's the peach and almond—"

"Rebecca Darden. Shut up about the fucking food and sit down," Rachel snapped. "We are going to talk about it."

Bec froze and sucked in a long breath. After a minute, she released it on a long exhale. "It's my fault," she said, sinking into a chair.

"No. It's absolutely not." Rachel sat across from her. "It's Preston's—"

"I went after him," Bec said. "You told me to leave it, to just get the divorce and forget the rest of it, but I didn't do that." Gray eyes sparkled with tears, but her words were clear. "I went after him with everything I had. I wanted to destroy everything that mattered, to *make him pay*. And I wanted to make his corrupt father to—"

She broke off and for the first time ever, Rachel saw Rebecca Darden, famed lawyer and corporate badass, cry.

"It's my fault," she wailed. "If I hadn't gone after Preston—"

Tears trailed Bec's face, and Rachel felt her own eyes water. Carefully, she pushed to her feet then limped back around the table and wrapped her good arm around her friend. "I'm glad you ignored me."

Bec pulled away.

"Look at you," she snapped. "How can you possibly be glad—?"

"Because Preston is *gone*. Because he doesn't have a hold over me any longer, because his father is no longer in a position of power. Or, at least, I'm assuming you got the asshole canned since you are Rebecca *fucking* Darden." A small smile tipped Bec's lips and she nodded. "I'm glad because they can't hurt anyone else."

Bec's chin dropped to her chest, and Rachel knew it would take time for her friend to see that she was okay, that she didn't blame her.

That it would take time for Bec to stop blaming herself.

"I know one conversation isn't a be-all-end-all, that you're a stubborn pain in the ass who likes to shoulder the burdens of everyone else and make them right," Rachel said. "But I don't blame you. I'll *never* blame you. And . . . if you forget that, I'll sit you down and yell at you until you remember."

A flash of white teeth as Bec glanced back up. "You're mean when you're on Molly's withdrawal."

"Good thing you bought half the menu, then." Moving gingerly, Rachel navigated her way back to the chair across from Bec.

Bec snorted. "I really did."

"I know." She grinned. "And I'm going to take a page out of Abby's book and say, you need to invest in waterproof mascara."

Her friend had serious raccoon eyes happening.

Bec groaned and wiped a finger under each eye, smearing the black smudges further. "This is why I hate feelings."

"This is why you hate things you can't control."

"Maybe."

They both laughed, which resulted in Rachel wincing and forbidding Bec from any jokes or sarcasm or pithy comments on the world at hand. Which, of course, meant they both spent their whole lunch doing all three.

Rachel very quickly learned how to laugh without hurting her ribs.

EPILOGUE

Sebastian

TWO MONTHS HAD PASSED, but waking up next to Rachel was still the best thing in the world.

Especially now that she'd had her cast taken off and her bruises had faded. Of course, she was still as stubborn as ever, declaring herself completely recovered, but he had seen the shadows under her eyes after sleepless nights, caught her wincing when she coughed or laughed and her ribs hurt. Though in truth, those moments were coming fewer and further between.

Thank God, because Bas didn't know how he'd have lived with himself if she hadn't gotten better.

But she had gotten better, and she'd bounced back remarkably quickly, poking fun at her injuries, declaring that all her hours of binging on Netflix was rotting her brain.

As if. The little stink had refused to listen to him and Heather and had been working from his apartment, almost from the moment she'd been able to get out of bed.

But he had to admit that despite moving so quickly from sex

to love to living together in just a few months time, he'd really enjoyed every minute of having Rachel in his space.

It had felt right—*she* had felt right from the first moment she'd smiled up at him at Bobby's.

The touch on his cheek startled him.

While he'd been daydreaming, the woman he loved had woken up and he'd missed his favorite thing in the world. The way she stretched upon waking—arching her back, arms extended, toes pointing, the soft groan that never failed to harden his morning wood into granite.

"Morning," she said softly.

"Morning, love." He bent down to kiss her forehead. "So, my cast-free girlfriend, what do you want to do today?"

"Besides shaving this Chewbacca leg?" She poked her foot out from beneath the covers, wiggled navy blue painted toes.

He slipped his hand down her back, cupping her ass and trailing his fingers across the hip that belonged to the *Chewbacca* leg. "I kind of like you hairy."

"Ew." She wrinkled her nose.

Bas kissed that cute nose. "So besides shaving, do you want to walk by the pier?"

She shuddered. "Too many tourists."

"Shopping?"

Rachel felt his forehead. "No fever. Have you been abducted by aliens?"

"What?" he said. "I love shopping with women."

Brown brows pulled down and together. "Women?"

"You," he hurried to say. "Only you. Other women are dead to me."

"Good." She smirked. "But shopping? Seriously?"

"Seriously." A shrug. "I would never turn down a fashion show. You parading through the changing room in sexy little outfits? Taking me back and closing the door, watching you come in the mirror as I ate you out."

Rachel's cheeks went a little pink and she fanned herself. "Whew. So, you've apparently thought about that?"

Bas's lips twitched. "Just a little bit."

Okay, *a lot*. As in he'd spent a lot of time over the last two months fantasizing about all the things he was going to do to Rachel when she was completely recovered.

"Mmm," she said and tilted her head to the side, considering. "I could actually get behind prancing around in cute little outfits for you. Granted, you have to buy more of that gorgeous lingerie and prance around in outfits of your own."

"You mean this bag of lingerie?" he asked, reaching a hand out of bed as if to reach under the mattress.

Her jaw dropped open. "What?"

"I'm kidding." He kissed her. "The bag's in the closet."

She snorted. "You are such a dork. But because you're my dork, I'm keeping you."

A grin tugged at his mouth. "So, no to shopping, yes to future mutual fashion shows, and no to the touristy spots. Where does that leave us?"

"Aren't you going to ask what my fantasy is?"

Well, that was a really good point.

He rolled to his back, tugging her so she was sprawled across his chest. Her hair bounced forward, tickling his face. He tucked the strands behind her ears and laughed when they bounced right back.

"It's impossible," she said, leaning forward and shaking her head, tickling him again. "This crazy mop doesn't cooperate, especially in the mornings."

"I like your crazy hair," he said, running his fingers through the strands.

"Maybe," she said.

The blanket slid down from her shoulders to her waist, affording a very nice view of her braless state. Fuck, but his mouth watered to taste them again.

"So, are you gonna leave your guy hanging?" he asked, his voice a little rough.

"Hmm?" Her fingers trailed down his bare chest, and he had to force himself to focus, to not yank her tightly against him and kiss her senseless.

"Your fantasy," he rasped when her fingertips teased the hem of his boxer briefs. "What is it?" Not the smoothest, but fuck, her breasts were in his face, her fingers were close to the motherland, and his cock was ready to break in half.

"Oh." She leaned close, pressing her breasts to his chest, tilting her chin up so that she could whisper in his ear. "My fantasy is for you to strip me naked and then spend the entire day making love to me."

He flipped their positions between one heartbeat and the next, her legs coming up to wrap around his hips.

"You sure?" Bas asked, his mouth a hairsbreadth away from hers.

"Yes, I'm sure. Please, Bas, stop worrying about me and all the shit that happened in the past. Let's . . . not forget it exactly, because I don't think that's possible." Her hands came to rest on his shoulders. "But can we stop making it the focus and center of everything and just move forward? If something hurts, I'll tell you. If I don't like something, I'll tell you." Her eyes locked with his. "And I hope to God you'll promise to do the same." She tilted her pelvis, pressing her pussy against the erection tenting his underwear. "But today—now—I'm healthy, I'm horny, and I need you inside me."

"I love you," he said. "You're so deeply sewn into my being that I don't think I could ever deny you anything."

Rachel's lips curved. "Those are dangerous words to tell a

woman." She tugged him down, mouths almost touching. "Also, I love you, so, so much."

He kissed her, and then they spoke in touches and caresses, in strokes of their tongues, in nips of their teeth, in brushes of their fingers, rather than words. He stripped off her tank top, slipped off her pajama bottoms, and then traced every part of her with his lips, his fingers, his tongue.

Bas memorized every freckle and scar, teased the spot behind her ear that never failed to make her shiver. He kissed down her sides, gentle over those still-healing ribs, down over her hips . . . and in between.

She writhed against his mouth, groaned when he slipped a finger inside, but then she pushed him roughly away.

"Not now," she gasped. "Not this time. I want you inside me, Bas. Please."

As if he could deny her anything.

He reached for the nightstand and withdrew a condom then slipped it on and pushed aside.

Fuck.

That was—she was—he was beyond ready to blow and in seriously dangerous territory.

"Baby?"

Bas peeled back his lids then promptly had to grit his teeth. Rachel was flushed, her lips kiss-swollen, her brown eyes liquid chocolate. "You okay, sweetheart?"

"Can you move now?"

Fuck yes, he could move.

He laughed, but that quickly turned into a groan when she squeezed some internal muscle that had stars flashing behind his eyes.

But he moved, dammit. He moved until she bucked against him, until she screamed his name and exploded around him, until he lost his battle with control and called out her name.

Collapsing next to her, Bas rolled to his side and pulled her close. Both of them were panting and covered in sweat.

"I'm out of . . . shape," she gasped.

"I have ideas how to fix that."

She snuggled close. "I bet you do. But this is *my* fantasy." She nipped at his jaw. "So, I'm giving you fifteen minutes to recover yourself, and then we're going for another set."

He pretended to consider that. "Workout instructor and disobedient student. I can work with that."

Rachel smacked his chest, but she was smiling, and Bas found that this start to the day, just waking up next to the person he loved, joking around with her, smelling the floral scent of her shampoo, watching her eyes warm as she looked up at him when he was just being himself, not some version of Sebastian he'd thought he needed to be, but just her *Bas* . . .

Yeah, he wanted to be Rachel's Bas more than anything else in his life.

More than a job.

More than any outside approval he'd thought he needed.

More than surpassing the ridiculous standards he'd set for himself.

He wanted this woman. Forever.

"I'm keeping you," he said.

"Oh yeah?" She pushed him flat on his back and straddled his hips, then adopted a really horrible Arnold Schwarzenegger accent while flexing a bicep. "You've been a bad boy."

"When does Arnold say that?" he asked, attempting to control his laughter.

"I'm improvising, okay?" She coughed, tried again. "I'll be back? It's not a tumor? Hasta la vista, baby?"

"Stop." Bas shuddered. "I take back the workout instructor fantasy. Immediately."

"It wasn't that bad." Rachel pouted then burst into giggles

when he just raised a brow and stared at her. "Okay, fine," she said. "It was horrible." And she was so adorably perfect that he couldn't resist kissing her all over again.

Love and laughter.

Yeah, he could build a life with that.

Thank you for reading! I hope you loved meeting Rachel and Bas! The next book in the Billionaire's Club series is BAD DIVORCE. Find out what happens when Bec's ex (who turns out not to be an *ex*) shows up on her doorstep...

CLICK HERE TO READ BAD DIVORCE NOW >

And if you enjoyed BAD HOOKUP, you'll love the sexy, sweet, and close-knit Breakers Hockey crew. The first book in the series, BROKEN, is now live!

The more she falls for Stefan, the more she risks her career... Don't miss the Gold Hockey series. It begins with the over 400 five-star-reviewed BLOCKED!

"Off-the-charts hot, smexy scenes with one of the best book boyfriends I have come across!" —Amazon reviewer

DOWNLOAD BLOCKED FOR FREE >

I so appreciate your help in spreading the word about my books, including sharing with friends! Please leave a review on your favorite book site!

You can also join my Facebook group, the Fabinators, for exclusive giveaways and sneak peeks of future books.

Excerpt from BAD DIVORCE

Bec closed the file she'd been working on and stretched her arms above her head. Her shoulders ached, her eyes burned—she gone way over the thirty minutes her optometrist recommended—and she was the absolute last person left in the building.

Seriously.

Security had come by her office an hour before, telling her they'd locked up and the high-rise was empty.

Except for her.

She probably should have been lonely, being the singular human presence around, but Bec loved this time of night. It was after one, she'd been in the office since six the previous morning working on a case that was preparing for trial.

But fuck, did she love finding a legal loophole in a contract and then being the one to decisively close it.

Nothing was better than that.

Not being made partner several months before. Not having a slew of paralegals whose job it was to go line by line through all the paperwork pertinent to her cases and find loopholes like the one she'd just spent hours scouring for. Not the money or the power.

Those were all intoxicating in many ways.

But still, nothing topped the law itself.

The different interpretations, the way it morphed from based on a court's or judge's decision, how it changed from year to year to year.

It was a constantly shifting spider's web—fragile and intricate and complex.

It made sense to her when so many other things in her world did not.

She logged off of her computer, grabbed a stack of files from her desk, shoved them into her briefcase, and then slipped on her suit jacket and black pumps.

Down the elevator, through the locked door to the garage, and into her car.

Quiet.

So quiet.

She'd grown up in New York—or at least spent enough of her formative years in the Big Apple for her accent to reflect her time there—and felt more comfortable in big cities. San Francisco was a nice one, but it had a definite sleepy time . . . or at least the district that her office was located in did.

Normally, she liked that, preferred it over the way New York had always buzzed with activity.

But Bec had been . . . feeling weird as of late.

She was used to city life—the expensive rents, the exhaust fumes that hung in the air at all hours of the day, the horns and sirens and screeching brakes.

But this quiet . . . fuck, did it hit her straight in the gut.

Or maybe it wasn't *quiet* so much as disquiet?

Bec was a simple woman. She didn't censor herself, didn't trouble over hurt feelings or someone's toes being stepped on. She took care of business in the quickest, most efficient way possible.

That was Rebecca Darden. What she was famous for—at least in the legal world.

No prisoners. Decisive. Smart as hell and not a fucking pushover.

She'd spent a lifetime studying and working and losing sleep and clawing and fighting and struggling against the pressures of being in a male-dominated field to become that woman.

And yet . . .

"Fuck," she muttered and turned on her car, making her way through the quieted city to her apartment. "I'm losing it."

Because she couldn't help but feel that now she'd finally met her goal of being partner, of being revered and feared and even sometimes reviled—all fine qualities in her opinion—that she was missing out on something.

There.

She'd said it.

She felt that somehow along the way of everything she'd missed *something*.

Unfortunately, she couldn't figure out what the fuck that *something* was.

A bigger challenge?

Nope. She'd taken on a case with impossible odds and had just that evening figured out how to win it.

Longer hours?

Hell no. At this point, she was paying for an apartment she was hardly ever in.

More money? No. She had an obscene amount.

Different friends?

No fucking way. Her group of women and now a few men were the shit. They kept her sane and laughed at her jokes and were really incredible people.

She loved them and that was saying something, coming from her and her limited tolerance of bullshit. She didn't like easy, let alone *love* easily.

And she loved every one of them.

So what?

That was the fucking problem. She *didn't* know. Normally, she'd just turn that particular puzzle over in her mind until she figured it out, as she'd done with the contract that evening.

But she'd been turning this freaking enigma over in her mind for months and Bec was no closer to discovering the exact source of her unease.

"Boo fucking hoo," she murmured, pulling into her parking spot and making it up to her floor via her private elevator.

The lift went directly to her penthouse—yes, the apartment she hardly spent any time in was a ridiculously expensive penthouse—and required a code to access it.

So Bec really didn't expect to see another person waiting for her when the doors opened with a soft *ding* and she stepped off.

But there *was* another person waiting just outside her front door.

A person she never expected to see again.

Luke Pearson.

Her ex-husband.

It was one-fucking-thirty in the morning, and her ex-husband was sitting on the floor outside her apartment.

Asleep.

Fuming, she marched over to him and kicked his shoe. Hard.

"Luke. Why in the ever loving fuck are you here?"

His lids peeled back and sleepy green eyes met hers. "Becky," he murmured. "You're gorgeous as always." The drowsiness began to fade from his expression. "Did you just come from work?" He glanced down at his phone. "Do you know what time it is?"

"Of course I know what time it is—" Bec bit back the words. Fuck, but wasn't this conversation an exact replica of the broken record one they'd had *way* too many times over the course of their relationship?

She crossed her arms. "Never mind that." A glare that had

withered balls much bigger than Luke's "Why did you break into my apartment?"

He stood. "First, I didn't break into your apartment. This is the hall. Second," he hurried to say when she opened her mouth to argue semantics, "I didn't break in. You used our anniversary as the code."

Oh for fuck's sake.

Well, she was changing that tomorrow . . . today . . . fuck, *yesterday*, now that—

"Go away, Luke," she said, pushing past him and unlocking her door while blocking his view of the keypad that was identical to that of the elevator. Her front door's code was not the date of her anniversary with her ex.

But Luke probably already knew that, given that he had been sitting on the floor of her hallway rather than on her couch, beer in hand, feet making prints on her glass coffee table.

Men.

Fucking men.

She slammed the door closed behind her and threw the dead bolt. The knock approximately one second later did not surprise her. Bec dropped her briefcase to the floor then opened it just enough to shoot angry eyes at him through the narrow gap the dead bolt allowed.

Serious green eyes fixed onto hers. "We need to talk."

"Luke," she snapped. "I'm exhausted. It's the middle of the night. I wouldn't have any patience to talk to my best friends right now, let alone my ex-husband."

"Funny story about that," he said, his lips curving. "Turns out that I'm not actually your *ex*-husband."

—BAD DIVORCE is out now!

Want a free bonus story? Hate missing Elise's new releases?
Love contests, exclusive excerpts and giveaways?
Then signup for Elise's newsletter here!
https://www.elisefaber.com/newsletter

And join Elise's fan group, the Fabinators https://www.
facebook.com/groups/fabinators for insider information, sneak
peaks at new releases, and fun freebies! Hope to see you there!

BILLIONAIRE'S CLUB

Bad Night Stand

Bad Breakup

Bad Husband

Bad Hookup

Bad Divorce

Bad Fiancé

Bad Boyfriend

Bad Blind Date

Bad Wedding

Bad Engagement

Bad Bridesmaid

Bad Swipe

Bad Girlfriend

Bad Bestfriend

Bad Billionaire's Quickies

Did you miss any of the other Billionaire's Club books? Check out excerpts from the series below or find the full series at https://www.elisefaber.com/all-books

---

Bad Night Stand
Book One
https://www.elisefaber.com/bad-night-stand

Abby

"I'M THE BEST FRIEND," I said and lifted my chin, forcing my words to be matter-of-fact. I'd been through this before. "You might be fuckable to the nth degree and perfect for Seraphina, but I refuse to set her up with a liar."

In a movement too quick for my brain to process, my stool was shoved to the side and I was pinned against the bar, heavy hips pressing into me, a hard chest two inches from my mouth.

Seraphina whipped around at the movement and I could just see her over Jordan's shoulder, her blue eyes concerned.

"Hi, Seraphina, I'm Jordan," he said, calm as can be, gaze locked onto my face then my eyes when mine invariably couldn't stay away. "I'm going to borrow your friend for a minute."

"Abs?" she asked, and I knew she'd go to bat for me right then and there if I needed her to.

"Weasel or no?" I managed to gasp out. For some reason, I couldn't catch my breath.

Not that it had anything to do with Jordan.

No, it had *everything* to do with him.

"Weasel?" he asked.

I shook my head, focused on my best friend. Weasel was our code name for the men trying to weasel, quite literally, their way into my pants and then into hers.

I was just about ready to say fuck it—or me, rather—even if Jordan was a Weasel. He smelled amazing. His body was hard and hot against mine.

And it had been way too long since I'd had sex.

"No chemistry on my part—" Seraphina began.

"Your friend isn't who I'm attracted to," Jordan growled out. "You are, and it's fucking pissing me off that you don't believe that."

—Get your copy at https://www.elisefaber.com/bad-night-stand

Bad Breakup
Book Two
https://www.elisefaber.com/bad-breakup

CeCe

"You're even more beautiful than I remember," he said, and the rough edges of his accent hacked at the words, making them more of a growl rather than a soft sentiment.

Her breath caught, and she found her eyes drawn to the stormy blue of Colin's.

And she stared again, utterly entranced before she remembered how it had all ended.

Her in a white dress.

Alone, except for the priest who'd given her a pitying look and invited her to stay as long as she needed.

But it had always been like this, Colin's gruff words winning her over. They were unexpected from him—he was typically so reserved and taciturn. And that compliment, freely given as it was, chipped away at any defenses she managed to erect.

The problem was that his words weren't always followed up by action. In fact, they were typically trailed by pain for her and fury for him.

The hurt of those memories—of Colin so angry, her so broken—helped shore up her resolve.

"Don't say things like that," she snapped and started to pop her earbuds back in. Her friends at home had filled her phone with a slew of romantic audiobooks and she decided that she much preferred fictional heroes at the moment.

At least if they broke their heroine's heart, it was only once.

Colin had already broken hers twice.

She wasn't looking for a round three.

—Get your copy at https://www.elisefaber.com/bad-breakup.

Bad Husband
Book Three
https://www.elisefaber.com/bad-husband

Heather

"I'm getting drunk," he said, but allowed her to pull him inside the car so that her driver could shut the door behind them.

"You're already drunk," she said.

He stiffened. "*More* drunk."

"Fine," she said, half-worried he was going to launch himself from the sedan. She'd never seen Clay like this. Usually he was so cold and uncompromising, impenetrable even under the toughest of negotiations. He was . . . well, he was typically as *Steele*-like as his last name decreed.

She wrapped her arm through his in order to prevent any unplanned exits from the vehicle and gave the driver the name of her favorite bar. "If you really want to drink, let's do it right."

And *then* she'd drop him at his hotel.

Except it didn't happen that way.

Yes, they hit the bar.

Yes, they drank.

Yes, they got plastered.

But then they woke up . . . or at least, *Heather* woke up.

Naked.

With a softly snoring Clay Steele passed out next to her in bed.

That wasn't the worst part.

Because Heather woke up naked and with a softly snoring Clay Steele in her bed *and* she was wearing a giant diamond ring on her left hand.

Still not the worst part.

That came in the form of a slightly crumpled marriage certificate tucked under her right cheek.

And not the one on her face.

She pulled it from beneath her, a cold sweat breaking out on her body, dread in every nerve and cell.

She *still* wasn't prepared for the horror she found.

The marriage license had been signed by . . . Heather O'Keith and Clay Steele.

Holy fuck, what had she done?

—Get your copy https://www.elisefaber.com/bad-husband.

Bad Divorce

Book Five
https://www.elisefaber.com/bad-divorce

Bec

"Boo fucking hoo," she murmured, pulling into her parking spot and making it up to her floor via her private elevator.

The lift went directly to her penthouse—yes, the apartment she hardly spent any time in was a ridiculously expensive penthouse—and required a code to access it.

So Bec really didn't expect to see another person waiting for her when the doors opened with a soft *ding* and she stepped off.

But there *was* another person waiting just outside her front door.

A person she never expected to see again.

Luke Pearson.

Her ex-husband.

It was one-fucking-thirty in the morning, and her ex-husband was sitting on the floor outside her apartment.

Asleep.

Fuming, she marched over to him and kicked his shoe. Hard.

"Luke. Why in the ever loving fuck are you here?"

His lids peeled back and sleepy green eyes met hers. "Becky," he murmured. "You're gorgeous as always." The drowsiness began to fade from his expression. "Did you just come from work?" He glanced down at his phone. "Do you know what time it is?"

"Of course I know what time it is—" Bec bit back the words. Fuck, but wasn't this conversation an exact replica of the broken record one they'd had *way* too many times over the course of their relationship?

She crossed her arms. "Never mind that." A glare that had

withered balls much bigger than Luke's "Why did you break into my apartment?"

He stood. "First, I didn't break into your apartment. This is the hall. Second," he hurried to say when she opened her mouth to argue semantics, "I didn't break in. You used our anniversary as the code."

Oh for fuck's sake.

Well, she was changing that tomorrow . . . today . . . fuck, *yesterday*, now that—

"Go away, Luke," she said, pushing past him and unlocking her door while blocking his view of the keypad that was identical to that of the elevator. Her front door's code was not the date of her anniversary with her ex.

But Luke probably already knew that, given that he had been sitting on the floor of her hallway rather than on her couch, beer in hand, feet making prints on her glass coffee table.

Men.

Fucking men.

She slammed the door closed behind her and threw the dead bolt. The knock approximately one second later did not surprise her. Bec dropped her briefcase to the floor then opened it just enough to shoot angry eyes at him through the narrow gap the dead bolt allowed.

Serious green eyes fixed onto hers. "We need to talk."

"Luke," she snapped. "I'm exhausted. It's the middle of the night. I wouldn't have any patience to talk to my best friends right now, let alone my ex-husband."

"Funny story about that," he said, his lips curving. "Turns out that I'm not actually your *ex*-husband."

—Get your copy at https://www.elisefaber.com/bad-divorce

Bad Fiancé
Book Six
https://www.elisefaber.com/bad-fiance

Seraphina

Sera was alone, pining after a man who'd created the latest social media craze.

Yup. Her life was *ah-maz-ing*.

Tate cleared his throat, and Sera realized she'd been staring at him dumbfounded for a good couple of minutes.

"I'm sorry, Mr. Conner." She stood, forcing herself to shake his hand. "I was woolgathering."

Sparks. The moment their skin touched, she felt *actual* sparks.

Just like every time before.

And just like every time before, she was the only one affected.

He smiled—eliciting more sparks, because her body was a stupid jerk—and said, "I've been known to do that from time to time."

Sera indicated for him to sit in the chair in front of her desk as she sank into her own chair. He continued to stand, but she started talking anyway, desperate to get this conversation over with. "How can I help you today?" she asked. "I do hope"—*Do hope? What was she, British? Ugh.*—"I-uh . . . I hope you were able to find a house. The agents I passed along are very good at finding unique properties, and I even gave them a few locations to start with . . . " She bit her lip, attempting to stop the ramble.

"No."

Just no.

Um. Okay.

He lifted a hand, rubbed the back of his neck. The movement made his shirt lift, exposing several inches of flat stomach and tan skin and, oh God, a trail of blond hair leading south. Her mouth watered, desperate to trace that path with her tongue—

Sera sucked in a breath, popped to her feet.

"Ah. I'm sorry." She picked up a random file, pretending to know what was in it. "I'm actually really busy, so this will have to continue another time."

Like never.

She rounded her desk, forced a smile. "Mr. Conner," she said when he didn't move. "I'll have my assistant schedule something soon."

"Seraphina."

She shivered at the sound of her name on his lips—soft, a little raspy, and deep enough to conjure all sorts of unhelpful fantasies in her mind.

Shaking herself, she moved to open the door.

Suddenly, Tate was there, hand on hers, body inches away, spicy scent inundating her senses.

Sera's breath caught. "What are you—?"

He seemed to be arguing with himself then finally, those piercing blue eyes locked onto hers. "I need you to marry me."

—Get your copy at https://www.elisefaber.com/bad-fiance

Bad Boyfriend
Book Seven
https://www.elisefaber.com/bad-boyfriend

"WHO IS IT THEN?" she asked through stiff lips.

Because it couldn't be. Her brother didn't know about them. She'd made sure of it. They'd kept things on the down-low and . . . then she'd nursed her broken heart two thousand miles away in college.

"Tanner."

Her gut twisted.

Double fuck.

And a shit for good measure.

"That's fine, right?" Bas asked. "You guys seemed to get along great." Concern rippled across his face. "Is there something wrong. Did—"

"No," she said quickly. "That's great. I'm sorry. I'm just preoccupied with my new project."

He grinned. "Always work with you."

She blew him a kiss. "You know it."

"Great. So you'll be paired up with him. And I know it's been a while, but he's coming into town next week to catch up." He tapped the roof of her car, took a step back. "You want to grab dinner with us?"

"I'd love too," she lied before getting into her car and with a wave that hopefully didn't show her dismay, Kelsey drove away.

Paired up with Tanner.

Been there, done that.

Got the souvenir broken heart.

Triple fuck.

—Get your copy at https://www.elisefaber.com/bad-boyfriend

Breakaway

Breakout

Checked

Coasting

Centered

Charging

Caged

Crashed

Gold Christmas

Cycled

Caught (February 1,2022)

Breakers Hockey (all stand alone)

Broken

Boldly

Breathless

Ballsy (April 26,2022)

Love, Action, Camera (all stand alone)

Dotted Line

Action Shot

Close-Up

End Scene

Meet Cute

Love After Midnight (all stand alone)

Rum And Notes

Virgin Daiquiri

On The Rocks

Sex On The Seats

Life Sucks Series (**all stand alone**)

Train Wreck

Hot Mess

Dumpster Fire

Clusterf*@k

Fubar (March 29,2022)

Roosevelt Ranch Series (**all stand alone, series complete**)

Disaster at Roosevelt Ranch

Heartbreak at Roosevelt Ranch

Collision at Roosevelt Ranch

Regret at Roosevelt Ranch

Desire at Roosevelt Ranch

Phoenix Series (**read in order**)

Phoenix Rising

Dark Phoenix

Phoenix Freed

Phoenix: LexTal Chronicles (**rereleasing soon, stand alone, Phoenix world**)

From Ashes

In Flames

To Smoke

KTS Series

Riding The Edge

Crossing The Line

Leveling The Field

Scorching The Earth (January 25,2022)

Cocky Heroes World

Tattooed Troublemaker

ACKNOWLEDGMENTS

This is always the point in the publishing process where I'm amazed by how many people have a hand in making sure that the characters and words bumping around in my head somehow make it onto the page in a semi-coherent state. My editors, Julie, Kay, and Christine, I literally could not do this without you (C, thanks also for working on your birthday on this one! You are amazing!). Hubs, you know how often I run crazy ideas and plot twists and character traits past you. Thanks for never brushing me off and for always lending that open ear. KC. Dude. You always offer the best advice and thank you for being my sounding board every *single* time. You're amazeballs. My fan group, my fabulous Fabinators, you keep me sane and ripe in character names when I brain fart (frequent and often) and I can't thank you enough for your support. And Heather, thanks for jumping headfirst into the PR boat on this one. I so appreciate you stepping up and diving in to support my books.

Last, but certainly not least, thank you, dear reader. Thank you for supporting my books, for loving the characters who are so dear to me, and for the messages and emails and reviews. They make the long hours, late nights, and *way* too early mornings worth it.

Love you guys!
—XOXO,
E

ABOUT THE AUTHOR

USA Today bestselling author, Elise Faber, loves chocolate, Star Wars, Harry Potter, and hockey (the order depending on the day and how well her team -- the Sharks! -- are playing). She and her husband also play as much hockey as they can squeeze into their schedules, so much so that their typical date night is spent on the ice. Elise is the mom to two exuberant boys and lives in Northern California. Connect with her in her Facebook group, the Fabinators or find more information about her books at www.elisefaber.com.

facebook.com/elisefaberauthor

amazon.com/author/elisefaber

bookbub.com/profile/elise-faber

instagram.com/elisefaber

goodreads.com/elisefaber

pinterest.com/elisefaberwrite